CU00922128

# Side Guys: It's Still Sex I Have Intercourse

*Non-Penetrative Sex Comes Out of the Closet*

"Queer men often feel so much shame for their sexual desires (or lack thereof). We feel like there are only a couple of 'proper ways' to have 'gay sex.' If we're not a power bottom with a juicy booty, a Dom top with a thick 8-incher, or a vers prince who flips easily in the sack—we're aberrations, not normal, not 'real gays.' Spoiler: that's far from the truth, and Dr. Kort knows this firsthand. By sharing his and others' experiences with being sides, Dr. Kort helps reveal the myriad of ways we can have pleasurable sex, all while removing shame from the equation."

Zachary Zane, Author of Boyslut:
A Memoir and Manifesto

---

"By coming up with 'sides,' Joe Kort gave gay men who don't enjoy anal sex a positive way to describe themselves — instead of having to tell other gay guys what they aren't (not a top, not a bottom, not vers), thanks to Joe these guys now get to tell other gay men what the are: they're sides."

Dan Savage, Sex and Relationship Columnist
and Podcaster

# About the Author

Psychotherapist Joe Kort, Ph.D., LMSW, is the clinical director and founder of The Center for Relationship and Sexual Health in Royal Oak, Michigan. He is a board-certified clinical sexologist, author of four books, lecturer and facilitator of therapeutic workshops. Throughout his 39 years of private practice, he successfully has utilized varying therapy modalities to help hundreds of individuals and couples improve their lives and strengthen their relationships.

Dr. Kort specializes in marital problems and conflicts; mixed orientation marriages; male sexuality and sexual health concerns; "sex addiction," out-of-control sexual behaviors; sexual identity issues; childhood sexual abuse; LGBTQIA Affirmative Therapy; and Imago Relationship Therapy.

He is trained in EMDR (Eye Movement Desensitization Reprocessing), a safe and effective treatment that can help patients who have suffered for years from anxiety, distressing memories, nightmares, insomnia, abuse or other traumatic events.

Dr. Kort obtained his undergraduate degree from Michigan State University in East Lansing, Michigan, with a dual major in psychology and social work. He earned master's degrees in social work and psychology from Wayne State University in Detroit, Michigan, and a doctorate (Ph.D.) in Clinical Sexology from the American Academy of Clinical Sexologists.

He has written numerous published journal and magazine articles and is a regular contributor to the online blog for Psychology Today. Dr. Kort is in his third season of Smart Sex, Smart Love, a podcast series featuring a variety of topics – from sexual health issues to parenting conflicts, men's health, sexuality as you grow old, marital problems, dating today, transgender concerns, kink, and much more (www.smartsexsmartlove.com).

Dr. Kort also conducts workshops and intensives for singles and couples.

His career focuses on advancing the social acceptance and professional treatment of issues surrounding sexual health as well as the gay, lesbian, bisexual and transgender communities.

Notice To Readers: This book is intended as a reference volume only. It is not a medical manual. The information contained in this book was written to help readers make informed decisions about their sexual practices and about health issues associated with sexuality. It was not designed as a substitute for any treatment that may have been prescribed by your personal physician. If you suspect that you have a medical problem, see a competent physician to discuss your concerns.

All authors included herein have given written permission allowing their stories to be published.

---

Side Guys: It's Still Sex Even if You Don't Have Intercourse
By Joe Kort, Ph.D.

Copyright © 2024 Joe Kort
All rights reserved.

No part of this book may be reproduced, stored in a retrieval system, or transmitted in any form or by any means—electronic, mechanical, photocopying, recording, or otherwise—without the prior written permission of the publisher, except for the inclusion of brief quotations in a review.

ISBN: [Your ISBN Number]

Published by "Smart Sex, Smart Love" Books
www.joekort.com

First Edition: October, 2024

Disclaimer:
This book is a work of non-fiction. While every effort has been made to ensure that the information contained herein is accurate, the author and publisher assume no responsibility for errors or omissions, or for damages that may result from the use of information contained in this book.

# Acknowledgements

So many people have helped and supported me in getting the term "side" out to the gay and bisexual male community. I could not have done this without your support and love to help me banish the shame I had for being a gay man who neither topped nor bottomed.

Thanks to John Mifsud, the friend who attended one of my workshops, and to whom I came out to as a "side" early on. He was so congratulatory on my bravery to be open about this.

Next, I want to thank the men who supported me to create the private Facebook group, Side Guys, which, at first, I was not going to do because I was so busy. Thank you Jason Villarreal for encouraging me to start the group and helping me get it off the ground. Without the generous help of facilitators, including Kerry Harding, Mike Crane, Buzz Charton, and Sparky Sikes, I could not have continued Side Guys, now growing by nearly 100 men a month. Additionally, I thank each and every man who is a member of Side Guys and shared their story and stated their relief from the shame of feeling different and isolated. You are not alone!

Many thanks to sex columnist Bobby Box who helped get out the word about sides.

Thanks also must go to Grindr and Scruff for adding "side" as a sexual preference so that none of us sides have to write in "no anal" and who now can feel that "sides" is a legitimate sexual style.

Also, I want to thank my longtime editor, James Townsend, for helping me put this book together. You make me sound so much better and accessible to the reader when you edit my work.

Finally, I want to thank my husband of 31 years, Mike Cramer, for honoring me as his side partner and being sides together. Your support of my work and my life is more than I ever thought I would get from anyone in my lifetime. You are the one and only love of my life.

Warmly,


Joe Kort, Ph.D.

From the original article on *Huffington Post*
Published April 16, 2013

## Guys on the 'Side': Looking Beyond Gay Tops and Bottoms

What if a guy isn't a top, a bottom or even versatile? What about gay men who have never engaged in anal sex and never will, ever? I think they deserve a name of their own. I call them "sides," and they typically struggle with tremendous feelings of shame.

By Joe Kort, Ph.D., Contributor
Certified Sex and Relationship Therapist

Gay men are constantly referring to and defining themselves as "tops" or "bottoms." When they consider dating or simply hooking up, gay men typically ask the other guy whether he's a top, a bottom or "versatile." It's important to find this out as soon as possible, because if you are planning to date or get into a relationship, it's vitally important that you and he be sexually compatible with each other.

The whole issue of tops and bottoms came up recently with the release of a new study that looked at whether or not people can determine whether a gay man is a top or a bottom just by looking at facial cues. The study revealed that judgments made about whether an individual is a top or a bottom are based on perceived masculine and feminine traits.

There's so much talk and discussion about who gives and who receives. I've had straight people tell me that they assumed that most gay guys simply take turns. Yes, some do, but most don't. But what if a guy isn't a top, a bottom or even versatile? What about gay men who have never engaged in anal sex and never will, ever?

I think they deserve a name of their own. I call them "sides."

### Defining a Side

Sides prefer to kiss, hug, and engage in oral sex, rimming, mutual masturbation and rubbing up and down on each other, to name just a few of the sexual activities they enjoy. These men enjoy practically every sexual practice aside from anal penetration of any kind. They may have tried it, and even performed it for some time, before they became aware that for them, it was simply not erotic and wasn't getting any more so. Some may even enjoy receiving or giving anal stimulation with a finger, but nothing beyond that.

### Sexual Shame and Masculinity

Sides typically struggle with tremendous feelings of shame. They secretly believe that they should be engaging in and enjoying anal sex, and that something must be wrong with them if they are not. Often they won't publicly admit to not engaging in anal sex, because of the judgments that other gay men might (and most likely will) make about them. I have heard gay men (and even straight people) say that if they aren't penetrating or being penetrated, they aren't having "real" sex.

If a man has undergone prostate surgery that caused nerve damage to the penis or suffers from hemorrhoids or other issues that make anal penetration impossible, uncomfortable, or unappealing, then that physiological or medical reason takes most of the shame out of being a side. These men may be genuine tops or bottoms but become sides out of necessity.

The gay male community has its own preferences that often slide into prejudices, and a great many look down on anyone who's not a top. Bottoms get talked about, even dismissed, as if they were women. As the joke goes, "Who pays for a gay male wedding? The father of the bottom." While that may be funny, it shows a cruel contempt for femininity. It makes the insensitive presumption that a man "takes the woman's role" by receiving, and that there's something wrong with him for it, namely that he's not masculine.

Straight men labor under the same misconception. If they enjoy anal stimulation for pleasure, they often worry that they might be gay. In my office I've heard straight men admit that they enjoy receiving anal penetration from sex toys, or by having their female partners strap on a dildo and give it to them. The slang term for that is "pegging," and many straight men love it. I jokingly tell the straight men who are insecure about enjoying anal play that, as a sex therapist, I am obliged to tell them that the human anus has no sexual orientation. The opportunity for anal pleasure exists in men and women alike, whether they are gay, bisexual, straight or of any orientation in between. Whether a man enjoys anal sex or not is no reflection on his sexual orientation, and if he's gay, it doesn't define whether or not he's "really" having sex.

Historically, lesbians were told that with no vaginal penetration, they were not having "real" sex (and even today, some still are told this). These erroneous judgments come from a heterosexist and patriarchal definition of the only "right" way to enjoy sex.

One problem with this rigid model (pun intended) is that as males age and begin to lose their ability to achieve a full, strong erection on demand, they fear that they will never have "sex" again. They must learn other ways to satisfy their partners. But in order to do so, they must first work through the misconception that the only good sex is penetrative sex.

**It's OK to Be a Side!**

It's high time for sides to come out and feel proud and secure about their sexuality. Not being a top or a bottom doesn't mean that one is less gay or less masculine. It doesn't make anyone any less of a sexual human being.

The internet is showing us that people get into a wide

variety of sexual pleasures, and whatever you get into is exactly right for you.

Given the freedom to experiment and explore new techniques, being a side becomes equally hot and exciting as being a top, a bottom or an aficionado of any other position or practice.

Come out and be the *side queen* you were meant to be!

# PART ONE

Back in 2013, I published the article (included here) in *The Huffington Post* in which I wrote that gay men are constantly referring to and defining themselves as "tops," "bottoms," or "versatiles" (otherwise known as "vers"). Some gay men even refer to themselves as "top vers," meaning they mostly top but sometimes will bottom and "bottom vers," meaning they mostly bottom but sometimes will top. These were the only categories offered for gay men on dating sites such as Grindr.

I always knew that I neither enjoyed nor wanted anal sex of any kind. I felt marginalized and had friends tell me I was a virgin because I never had "sex" simply because I never engaged in intercourse or penetration of any kind. So, I asked: "What if a guy isn't a top, a bottom or even vers? What about gay men who have *never* engaged in anal sex and never will, ever? I think they deserve a name of their own. I call them 'sides,' and they typically struggle with tremendous feelings of shame."

When I coined the term, I didn't realize how many gay men didn't enjoy topping or bottoming in the gay male community. I, myself, felt alone an outsider just like the others. We didn't have a community or sense of belonging.

Penetrative sex is the gold standard in both the straight and the LGBTQ worlds. Most people believe if you are not having intercourse then you're not having sex.

In our largely sexually repressed heteronormative Western culture, there is a longstanding concept of "normal sex." Until the LGBTQ community got angry at this repression and began to come out in force decades ago, very few people recognized sex between same-sex couples as something normal. Indeed, many still don't. Cultural values, whether they're right or wrong, usually take a very long time to change and mostly take the "two steps forward, and one step back" route, with every step toward progress being met with backlash.

# Why I Introduced the term, 'sides'

*"When it comes to sex, the most uncomfortable people in the room have all the power."*
*- Doug Braun-Harvey, Certified Sex Therapist*

Braun-Harvey's powerful statement couldn't be truer. Those who are the most uncomfortable around sexual and erotic issues often try to hijack conversations and talk about certain acts and behaviors as pathological or move the discussion to non-consent and the horrors and abuses of sex. So, it holds true that it not only includes people in the room, but also communities, therapists, religions, and anything else that wants others to be uncomfortable around sexuality because *they* are.

Unfortunately, people in the gay male community are subject to much of the same misconceptions and stereotyping as the rest of society. Too often gay men are subjected to the same narrowly drawn boundaries and their sexual activities are considered to some degree as being not "normal" or "not real sex."

If you're a "side" you probably have heard these comments from other gay men:

"*What?* You don't like getting anal?"

"What's wrong with you?"

"Were you traumatized or something?"

"What *do* you do then?"

"You are still a virgin?"

"That's just internalized homophobia"

"You're just afraid of getting HIV"

"So you're boring in bed?"

"You are immature, stunted and emotionally unevolved"

"Well, you just haven't had a really good fucking yet! Just wait until your prostate gets massaged out, then you'll see."

There are many reasons why someone—gay or straight—

may not enjoy or even be able to have penetrative sex. In a Daily Beast article acknowledging the importance of the introduction to the word "Sides," sex columnist Bobby Box cites a few of these: erectile difficulties, health issues, body image issues, performance anxiety, pain, vaginismus, fear of STIs, past trauma, pregnancy, vaginal dryness. For these reasons, penetration becomes a restrictive, harmful, and illogical way of regarding such a nuanced subject like sex.

Box notes that, "Penetration being the defining sexual act is nothing more than a religious response to reproduction, which, paired with a lack of pleasure-based sex education, then became part of the secular culture. By challenging these norms, sides open our minds to other sexual opportunities and mindsets where we create a larger, more inclusive space to play in."

It's so difficult for some gays to imagine that you don't engage in anal penetration they can't even hear it without pathologizing it … or not hearing it at all. But "side" sex is just as "normal" as everything else, despite what others say.

Let me share here some of the things I often hear from clients about "normal sex":

- Penetration is the "gold standard" of sex. Everything else is just foreplay.
- In the gay male community if you're a "top'" you're seen as the masculine one. If you're the "bottom," you're seen as the more feminine one. If you're a "versatile" you can go either way—but often assumed to really be a bottom.
- "Having sex" only means penetration.
- You're not having real sex if you don't have an orgasm.
- Lesbians don't really have "sex" because there's no penile penetration.
- You're only masculine if you're the one doing the penetration.

In his 2019 thesis, *The way of the world: How heterosexism shapes and distorts male same sexuality*, Ronald Hellman cites dozens of studies dating all the way back to 1917 showing that among the populations of men who have sex with men, those who preferred or engaged in penetrative sex *are in the minority*. He contends that the cultural stereotype of penetrative gay male sex contributes to "the marginalization and oppression of sexual minorities while leaving the public uninformed and subject to personal beliefs and prejudices regarding male same-sexual behavior."

In another 2019 paper, Angelo Bollas argues that "… stigmatisation of non-penetrative sexual practices is not only common in conservative heterosexual contexts. It is also observed among [men who have sex with men], possibly because erotic activity is based on heteronormative paradigms. Lack of erotic identity literature and education discourages people from not imitating and reproducing penile-vaginal intercourse as a prototype for all sexual practices. Thus, homosexism might emerge from heteronormative assumptions … but it has evolved into a homonormative practice whereby certain practices within non-heterosexual communities are to be associated with shame while others are celebrated as the norm."

We will see plenty of examples of this in the second part of this book, as men who have come out as "sides" recount their experiences of reckoning when they went against the cultural expectations of gay communities.

### Why I didn't attribute 'side' to the rest of the LBTQ communities

I was approached by a trans woman of color who was disappointed with me for not being inclusive with the term "side." I asked her if she could imagine what the response from the LBTQ community would be if I—a white, cisgender gay male—created a term for anyone other than gay men. Her contemptuous face reverted to a smile, and she agreed. We both knew that it would be met with comments like, "You're not a part of my community so don't be speaking for it, let alone invent terms for me or my community." I hear this all the time, so I didn't.

I was thrilled when Kerri Colby, an American trans performer and trans woman from Rupaul's Drag Race, tweeted, "I was today years old (sic) when I learned that I don't identify as a top or a bottom. But as a side," adding that she would spread the term to the rest of the LGBT community.

That being said, anyone can be a side. Anyone. Even those in the straight community can identify as a side as it simply refers to those individuals who are not interested in penetrative sex. The term is called, "outercourse" which is everything else we do sexually in bed instead of intercourse, which I discuss in the next few paragraphs.

### What a 'side' is not

Many people think that a side is asexual, abstinent, or nonsexual. Their immediate reaction to the term is that the person *is not* engaging in "sex," which they only think of as penetrative sex. This is a cultural myth that may have started with Bill Clinton. Clinton was president in 1995 and was asked if he had had sex with an intern, Monica Lewinsky. His now-famous answer was, "I did not have sex with that woman." In fact, he did. It was later discovered that she gave him a blow job. Oral sex *is* sex. It even has the word "sex" in it. However, he was trying to skirt the issue, or actually thinking that only intercourse was real sex.

I hear this all the time from my clients of every gender and sexual orientations. When I do a sexual history during their intake, I ask about sexual activity with partners.

Inevitably, if they're not having intercourse, they tell me they are not having sex. I must ask, then, if they are doing anything else, which they often are. Then I let them know that they are having sex.

## What is 'normal' sex, though?

After nearly 40 years of being a therapist specializing in sexual issues, I can tell you with conviction that there is no such thing as "normal sex." I could write volumes on what I've learned people do in the privacy of their bedroom … or in other places! There are as many ways to have sex as there is imagination.

Even so, as a gay male subject to the same cultural misconceptions I too was for many years ashamed to admit that I had never engaged in penetrative sex and that I never would. Then during a conference, I was talking with some colleagues about "tops" and "bottoms," and outed myself for being a gay man who doesn't engage in anal intercourse, and I joked, "Boxes have a bottom, a top, why can't men like me be *sides*? Why don't we have sides in this discussion?" We all laughed, but I got to thinking about this later and realized I was tired of feeling guilty, as though I was an oddball because I've *never* had penetrative sex. People even called me a "virgin" because I wasn't into anal, and it felt to me like an insult. Being a "top" or "bottom" or "vers" were the only acceptable models in the gay community, and I felt dissed for not fitting into the mold. Bottoms get talked about, even dismissed, as if they aren't men but rather are women.

This emphasis on "masculinity" as being superior and "femininity" being inferior or even "weak" is hardly surprising since we've been living under patriarchal rules for centuries. Straight men labor under the same misconception. If they enjoy anal stimulation for pleasure, they often worry that they might be gay. In my office I've heard straight men admit that they enjoy receiving anal penetration from sex toys, or by having their female partners strap on a dildo and give it to them. The slang term for that is "pegging," and many straight men love it.

### Your anus doesn't have a sexual orientation

I jokingly tell the straight men who are insecure about enjoying anal play that, as a sex therapist, I am obliged to tell them that the human anus has no sexual orientation. The opportunity for anal pleasure exists in men and women alike, whether they are gay, bisexual, straight or of any orientation in between. Whether a man enjoys anal sex or not is no reflection on his sexual orientation, and if he's gay, it doesn't define whether he's "really" having sex.

In the same way I tell gay men that just because you are not into anal sex doesn't mean you are any less gay. I have had countless closeted men in my office tell me they didn't think they were gay because they didn't want nor enjoy anal sex.

As I've said and taught for many years, sex is what *you think sex is*, not what someone else says it is.

### Outercourse

Although the term "sides" was coined for gay men who aren't into penetration, the term "outercourse" has been around for a while longer and can apply to anyone who, for myriad reasons, may not want to engage in penetrative sex. For instance:

You want intimacy but don't want to get pregnant or contract an STI.

One partner may have had a bad experience or trauma, or physically may not be able to have intercourse. Post-menopausal women, for example, may find vaginal intercourse too painful, and some men may not be able to get an erection.

A couple wants to learn more about what their partner likes

and does not like. Outercourse gives them an opportunity to explore their pleasures.

One or both partners may not be ready to have intercourse.

They may want to wait until marriage to have intercourse. Or they want to understand their own body more before having intercourse.

Many view penetrative sex as the main source of pleasure and are worried about their "performance." Outercourse takes the pressure off and couples can enjoy orgasms without penetrative sex.

They don't have to fake it. Some couples feel they must have an orgasm when having intercourse or their partner won't be satisfied. Outercourse can relieve this worry and free them to enjoy sex without pressure. In fact, studies have shown that building arousal through outercourse can stimulate an orgasm and one that is mind blowing.

The variety of sexual pleasures available to couples practicing outercourse and those men who are sides is nearly endless. For instance:

- Dry humping: rubbing genitals against each other often while still wearing clothes.
- Kissing: this can be a simple, fun, and very erotic activity.
- Mutual masturbation: partners can touch each other at the same time (Also is a great activity over the phone).
- Massage: rubbing, stroking, and exploring your partner's body with your hands can be extremely erotic. Add some scented candles and mood music and the rest will just happen.
- Tribadism (also known as scissoring). Two women can stimulate each other by rubbing their genitals against each other.
- Using vibrators and other sex toys is a great way to

reach orgasm without intercourse.
- Fingering: some may consider these "intercourse" because the vagina or anus is being penetrated. However, others find it a pleasurable outercourse activity.
- Oral sex
- Talking about fantasies can increase your sexual satisfaction, build intimacy, and even lead to an orgasm. This can include talking about any erotic fantasies you have from vanilla to BDSM or other fetishes.
- Even just sleeping in the nude or touching and caressing each other's bodies can bring so much pleasure.
- Taking a shower together and discovering water stimulation.
- Hand jobs.

Many would call these sexual practices immature and "not real sex." This is a shame because they are limiting themselves to intercourse only and believing everything else is foreplay or afterplay which minimizes the pleasure of outercourse.

## Defining 'side'

Sides prefer to kiss, hug, and engage in oral sex, rimming, mutual masturbation and rubbing up and down on each other, to name just a few of the sexual activities they enjoy. These men enjoy practically every sexual practice aside from anal penetration of any kind. They may have tried it, and even performed it for some time, before they became aware that, for them, it was simply not erotic and wasn't getting any more so. Some may even enjoy receiving or giving anal stimulation with a finger, but nothing beyond that.

# Sexual shame and masculinity

Sides typically struggle with tremendous feelings of shame. They secretly believe that they should be engaging in and enjoying anal sex, and that something must be wrong with them if they are not. Often, they won't publicly admit to not engaging in anal sex, because of the judgments that other gay men might (and most likely will) make about them. I have heard gay men (and even straight people) say that if they aren't penetrating or being penetrated, they aren't having "real" sex.

If a man has undergone prostate surgery that caused nerve damage to the penis or suffers from hemorrhoids or other issues that make anal penetration impossible, uncomfortable or unappealing, then that physiological or medical reason takes most of the shame out of being a side. Such an under-researched phenomenon known as anodyspareunia, which is having pain during receptive intercourse, either anal or vaginal. I would hazard a guess that it is under-researched because it's often thought of as a gay male problem or a woman's problem, and thus not taken seriously. My friend and colleague, Edward Angelini-Cooke, Ph.D., wrote his dissertation on the topic (See citations).

The gay male community has its own preferences that often slide into prejudices, and a great many look down on anyone who's not a top. Bottoms get talked about, even dismissed, as if they were women. As the joke goes, "Who pays for a gay male wedding? The father of the bottom." While that may be funny to some, it shows a cruel contempt for femininity. It makes the insensitive presumption that a man "takes the woman's role" by receiving, and that there's something wrong with him for it, namely that he's not masculine.

Straight men labor under the same misconception. If they enjoy anal stimulation for pleasure, they often worry that they might be gay. In my office I've heard straight men admit that they enjoy receiving anal penetration from sex toys, or by having their female partners strap on a dildo and give it to them. The slang term for this is "pegging," and many straight men love it. I jokingly tell the straight men who are insecure about enjoying anal play that the same thing I tell gay men who don't like anal play—your anus doesn't have a sexual orientation. The opportunity for anal pleasure exists in men and women alike, whether they are gay, bisexual, straight, or any orientation in between. Whether a man enjoys anal sex or not is no reflection on his sexual orientation, and if he's gay, it doesn't define whether or not he's "really" having sex.

Historically, lesbians were told that with no vaginal penetration, they were not having "real" sex (some are told this even today). These erroneous judgments come from a heterosexist and patriarchal definition of the only "right" way to enjoy sex.

One problem with this rigid model (pun intended) is that as males age and begin to lose their ability to achieve a full, strong erection on demand, they fear that they will never have "sex" again. They must learn other ways to satisfy their partners and themselves with a partner. But, to do so, they must first work through the misconception that the only good and pleasurable sex is penetrative sex.

### Our eroticism evolves

Couples, gay or straight or mixed orientation, may have tried anal and even performed it for some time before they became aware that, for them, it was simply not erotic and wasn't getting any more so. Some may even enjoy receiving or giving anal stimulation with a finger or sex toy, but nothing beyond that.

Like the person who did anal only because he was in love and gradually got real and admitted that they didn't like doing it anymore, our eroticism *evolves*. What we may have found exciting or even naughtily rebellious at age 20 can change to something different years later. Humans are adventurers by nature. We can easily become bored playing the same games, walking the same paths, engaging in the same old style of sex. We're not likely to sit at a table full of delicious breakfast dishes and just eat oatmeal, are we? We crave new tastes and different smells. Our sexuality is like that, too.

Consider, for instance, the aging man or one who has had prostate troubles and no longer can or will do anal even if he wants to. His sex life may even be richer and more enjoyable by engaging in the thousand other available erotic activities. What about the person who fears anal sex because of the AIDs virus? Does he have to give up having sex because anything else isn't "real?"

### From losing your virginity to discovering your sexual debut

Sadly, the expression "losing your virginity" is from Puritan culture and often refers to your first time with PIV (penis in vagina) or PIA (penis in anus). People's first experiences with either of these can be awkward, painful and even be from a sexually abusive situation. So why call that your "first time" rather than your "first intercourse experience?"

As sex therapists, we ask, "What was your sexual debut" so that you can identify *your* first pleasurable sexual experience. This takes the pressure off one act. It also opens people's minds that outercourse and side experiences are sex!

I worked with parents of an 18-year-old young man whose OnlyFans account was discovered by his parents where their son was showing off his feet and masturbating. They said to me, "We wanted our son's first time to be special" and I replied, "What makes you think this is his first time? While he is being sexual, that doesn't mean that what he is doing is 'special' to him."

## Finding other 'sides'

Before writing the 2013 article I searched around everywhere I could think of online for someone using the term "sides," and found nothing. But afterward the term started getting spread around and I found my inbox filled with hundreds of emails I was getting from guys telling me how grateful they were that someone validated their sexual behavior, how it made them feel empowered. Sometime in 2021 I formed a Facebook group called "Side Guys" that now has grown to nearly 8,000 members worldwide, and some of the guys in the group started petitioning Grindr to add "side" to their list of preferred positions and filters. Apparently, Grindr took them seriously, and they added it as a sexual position to their app. Now those men who do not engage in intercourse can self-identify as a "side." In our Facebook group, men are proudly posting their new status on Grindr. Scruff soon joined in adding "side" to their sexual preferences. Recently I've discovered that the term is being used in countries around the world in their own languages … and I couldn't be prouder. In October of 2023, I even was cited in the New York Times article, *Eight Sex Myths that Experts Wish Would Go Away: Equating sex with penetration also leaves out people who have sex in other ways*. For instance, Joe Kort, a sex therapist, has coined the term "sides" to describe gay men who do not have anal sex.

In 2022 gay publications such as Metrosource.com began to catch on and let the wider public know about the new term. Mike Henry, the talented comedian and sex educator who uses humor to teach, even created a humorous short video around the "sides" theme.

# The history of 'sides'

Being a "side" isn't something new. It's been around forever but we just didn't have a term to describe it in the gay community. By the 1980s the term "outercourse" began being used to describe sexual activity that doesn't involve vaginal or anal penetration. It largely gained popularity due to the growing awareness that people needed to practice safe sex and was mostly applied to heterosexual couplings. Back in 2011 an article was published in the *Journal of Sexual Medicine* in which researchers surveyed 25,000 gay and bisexual men in America about their most recent sexual encounters, and only 36 percent said they had bottomed, and 34 percent said they had topped. That means that nearly 65 percent of gay and bisexual men didn't have intercourse as part of their most recent sexual experience. The lead author of the study, Joshua Rosenberger, said, "Of all sexual behaviors that men reported occurring during their last sexual event, those involving the anus were the least common."

According to this research, we "sides" can see that we were in the majority!

## Another Label adding to the LGBTQIA?

I can practically hear the groans out there, people saying, "What? Another name? This is getting out of hand!" But think about it. Terminology always evolves as we discover more. We wouldn't use a medical manual from the 1950s or before when researching how to treat a problem. Leeches or lobotomies anyone? The more we discover, the more we come up with new names for things, and this is true of sexuality as well.

Since "sides" has been acknowledged out there, people have added to the definition and naming many sub-varieties in the category. A side can be a cisgender male, a transgender male (transman), or an intersex male. In addition, a side can be a masculine male, or a feminine male, a nonbinary male, or an androgynous male.

Furthermore, a side can be a gay male, a bisexual male, a pansexual male, or fall under the "ace" umbrella (asexual male/graysexual male/demisexual male, etc.).

A side can have multiple sub-descriptions. For example: a 100% Power Dom Frot Side.

Here are some further descriptions:

- 100% Side—A side who may have engaged in anal sex or anal play in the past, but now prefers to exclusively engage in non-penetrative sex.
- Power Side—A side who likes taking charge of a sexual situation. In addition, he can even be dominant (Power Dom Side), submissive (Power Sub Side), or versatile (Power Vers Side/Power Switch Side). See below for Dom/Sub/Switch/Vers Side definitions.
- Dom Side—A side who prefers to be dominant during sex.
- Sub Side—A side who prefers to submit, i.e., to be dominated.
- Switch Side—A side who may be a dom with one partner, and a sub with another (or even with the same partner).
- Frot Side—A side who likes to engage in frottage: male-to-male sexual activity that usually involves direct penis-to-penis contact. It can involve one's hand, trying to bring the two together for pleasure, but isn't always a necessity in the act.
- Top Side—A side who prefers the insertive role in occasional anal play or anal sex. In addition, he can even be a dom (dominant) top side, or a sub (submissive) top side, or a switch top side (switching between being dominant and submissive).
- Bottom Side—A side who prefers the receptive role

in occasional anal play or anal sex. In addition, he can even be a sub (submissive) bottom side, or a dom (dominant) bottom side, or a switch bottom side (switching between being dominant and submissive).

- Vers Side—A side who has no preferences regarding anal sex role in occasional anal play or anal sex.
- Side-ish/Demi Side/Sometimes a Side/Mostly a Side—A side who occasionally engages in anal sex or anal play.
- Oral Side—A side who likes oral sex. This can include blowjobs (fellatio), rim jobs (analingus), and/or cunnilingus (in the case of pre-op or no-op transmen, or sides who are bisexual/pansexual).
- Orthodox Side—A side who has never engaged in anal sex or anal play in the past.

So, all of us sides out there, take a victory lap and stand tall (or lie down) for who you are! And don't let anyone tell you that you're a "virgin" or aren't having "real" sex. You're a "Side Guy."

Although sides' fear of judgment from the gay community still exists, the addition of the term to sites like Grindr and Metrosource.com is a sign that more progressive ideas are beginning to breach the walls of ignorance and prejudice in the LGBTQ world. The more we talk about it and acknowledge that there are as many ways to have and enjoy sex as we can imagine, the less those of us who are sides will feel excluded or ashamed of their sexual practices.

To that end, I'm grateful for the many members of the "Side Guys" Facebook group who have told their stories. That the group appears to be growing daily is a hopeful sign of a more inclusive future.

As a therapist, I tell all my side guys that this is the most important thing: Communication is key when engaging in any sexual activity. Knowing expectations and boundaries, what you like and don't like, and what feels good and leads to an orgasm is key to a successful sexual relationship.

Take a lesson from the early days of your relationship when you spent a lot of time touching each other in erotic ways before engaging in intercourse. Those times were pretty hot and heavy, weren't they?

Whatever you do, don't abandon your erotic life. You are not alone, and now that our terminology and discussion is expanding, you have many more opportunities to find a partner who will celebrate your style of eroticism without penetration.

Keep reading and take heart from the following stories I've heard from the Side Guys Facebook Group who are finally standing tall for who they are.

# PART TWO

### 'You're Not Alone'
### Real Stories from Men on Facebook's 'Side Guys' Group

These are just some of the stories from men from around the world who've contacted me since I started the "Side Guys" Facebook group. Most have asked that I not use their real names for fear of being shamed, so I have honored their request. Meanwhile, I'd like to start with my own story.

### Creating a Three-Month Rule

I was born in 1963 so I grew up in the 1970s. I began masturbating when I was 11 years old, doing it compulsively until I sometimes would bleed. Scabs would form but I would masturbate anyway. I didn't know much about what was happening to me but I know I enjoyed myself immensely. I never imagined anal sex or anything anal at all, mine, or anyone else's. I always enjoyed the thought of giving oral sex and pleasing another guy. I also had some strong kinky fantasies but again, nothing included anal.

When I was 15 years old I discovered that a local bookstore sold gay erotica and porn, including *Honcho, Blueboy, Numbers,* and *Playgirl.* I knew I couldn't buy them so I'd sneak them into another bigger magazine like *Billboard Magazine* and buy that magazine. I'd ride my bike home and masturbate to the images in these magazines for hours, and then the next month I'd return to the bookstore to do it all over again. I don't remember any images of anal sex or any form of buttplay. If such images were in these magazines (not *Playgirl* of course) then I must have skipped over them because they didn't at all arouse me. I also knew I was not into the leather or jockstraps featured in these magazines. I just enjoyed men in underwear and naked and often focused on the flaccid penises that you'd always see in *Playgirl*. Between all this and my kinky interests, I knew as a teen what I wanted and what I didn't want. I was clear.

When I went off to college in 1981 I went to my first gay bar. I remember a guy lighting my cigarette and telling me that if I had a small dick I would have to be a bottom and if I had a big dick I would be the top. I didn't know what top and bottom meant, but I did know the size of my dick and once I understood what a top and bottom was it didn't matter what my size was—I was out, no interest at all. It wasn't that it disgusted me or turned me off, it just didn't turn me on. I had so many other sexual interests that were both kink and vanilla that I was satisfied with how I was.

I must have had over 500 sexual encounters at college as I would meet guys at the student union and restrooms and gave countless blowjobs. I was in my glory! Not to be confused with glory hole as I was not into those. I always wanted to see the guys I was sucking off. Plus, I always wondered who came in with a drill and made those holes in the bathroom for peep shows. But I digress.

Then the AIDS crisis came. People all around me started getting sick and dying. I was freaked out! Over time we learned that anal sex provided the highest rate of transmission and I remember being grateful I was not into that. People always ask me if it could be because of the AIDS crisis that I don't want anal sex. The answer is no.

When I was in my 20s I started dating guys. I never had more than one or two dates. Looking back, I wonder if it might have been because I didn't do anal sex. I didn't pay much attention to it at the time. My dating was not serious. It was just for fun as I was getting my degrees and focusing on becoming a therapist. Porn and masturbation was enough for me. The occasional hookups involved blowjobs and my kink.

Then in my mid 20s I became more serious about dating. Guys were more overt about wanting anal sex. I was honest and up front that this was not for me and was not going to happen. They would ask me, Why? Are you worried about AIDS? Maybe if you try it you'll like it. Did something happen to me?" The answer always was "No, I'm just not into it," and so they'd move on. I was very strong in this stance. I felt a little bit of shame that I didn't top or bottom, but not enough to try.

I also developed a rule around dating guys. I never liked dating a guy, having sex with him, and then having him ghost me or move on. I didn't care if hookups did that, but when it was a guy I dated it hurt me. So, I created a three-month rule. I wouldn't engage in anything sexual for the first three months. If a guy was not open to that then he wasn't for me. Some really nice guys, nice husband material, passed me by both because of my three-month rule and no anal.

Then I met Mike. He was willing to wait. He was not interested in anal sex. We dated. We slept together in our underwear. We kissed and held each other. And after three months we created our own sex life together that didn't include anal sex.

Thirty years later we're both happy and going strong.

**- Joe Kort**

### Tried It All

My journey with my sexuality has been challenging. I used to be jealous of people who were so sexually confident and knew themselves in that department. It was hard enough to come out as gay when I was 17-18 years old, let alone coming out as a side as a 32-year-old!

In college, I started to explore my sexuality with men. Learning from sexual partners and trying things out with my boyfriends. It took me a little longer to understand sexual positions because I wasn't really putting myself out there. I grew up Catholic, so I was always trying to be "virtuous" (whatever that meant for a "gay"). I knew I wanted to attract men, but I usually got shy when things started to get physical. Don't get me wrong—I've always had a strong sexual drive. I was turned on by so many men, and still am. I always sought emotional and physical intimacy. But I'd usually get tripped-up mentally trying to accommodate their expectations of me while still finding the experience pleasurable for myself. In other words, I was much more of a giver than a receiver in love. That's not a euphemism—I'm just speaking energetically—and I didn't know what turned me on. I have a nice ass, so most guys were interested in topping me. So, I tried bottoming. Like many, I found it painful. But I knew it wasn't supposed to be. It took some practice before I got to the point where bottoming was at least semi-pleasurable. But it was so much prep work! And even at its best, it was just intensely "meh."

I've also tried topping. For example, one of my boyfriends enjoyed the submissive role, and I wanted to offer him that experience. But each time I topped him I just wasn't into it. It was squishy and warm, which was nice—but turn me on it did not. I tried using pills to help make up for my lack of arousal, but even with pills there needs to be some level of sexual stimulation. Topping, to me, was the arousal equivalent to mixing cake batter. Comforting, but not sexy. I had no wish to dominate or be dominated. And so, it started to dawn within my most private and personal thoughts that maybe something was wrong with me. For this reason, the question from men on dating apps: "What are you into?" has always brought me anxiety. Even as I write that, it makes me sad because I know it was due to a lack of self-love, and me feeling like I didn't deserve to receive the kind of touch I really wanted. I have held a lot of shame about my body and being gay... and although I have much better self-esteem today, it's been a hard-learned lesson.

One of the biggest burdens on my heart has been a

belief that my subconscious came up with a long time ago: *If topping doesn't bring me pleasure, and neither does bottoming, then I am useless as a gay man.* All that struggle to come out, alienate my family, and break relationships ... what was it all for if I was just going to end up alone anyway? I spent years believing that ... And it made me feel as hopeless for my future as I did back when I was 13 and first struggling with the realization that I was gay. This belief limited how much love I could receive from others. When my gay friends (and most of my friends are gay) told me that I was a catch, all I could think was "Yeah, but they don't know I'm basically worthless in bed, which means worthless as a partner." I hid those sad feelings. And I avoided any questions of whether I was a "top," or "bottom." PS: Did you know that gays are *obsessed* with that question?

Fast forward to a day last year when I stumbled upon an article about "Gay Sides." I learned that there were other guys who weren't into anal penetration. And not only that, but they were also dealing with that same kind of shame and low expectations from love. Man, that has done so much for me. I joined the Facebook group, where I started to see the faces of other sides. They looked like normal guys. Many of them were hot as fuck! I started reading the stories of others around the world that were confused. And lonely. And searching ... just like me. Gay men who had so much love to give but couldn't find a person who would accept it. I started to learn that there are sides who, like me, had a lot of sexual experience with topping and bottoming, and just decided it wasn't worth the effort. That there are sides who have never tried anal, and don't care to. There are sides who are exclusively oral. There are sides who are bisexual. There are sides who are sometimes into topping! There are all kinds of sides! Just like there are all kinds of tops and bottoms. This knowledge brings me great joy. But more than that, it brings me hope that the more this term is understood and accepted, the higher likelihood that

I'll find a guy that's compatible with me. A guy who will ask me the question, "What are you into?" and smile with relief at my response.

**- Craig**

## Sides for 20 Years

I imagine that my story will be like others but hope that it may resonate with those who may not be where I am in life. As a very young 53-year-old, I'm so grateful that we have the word "side" to round out our identities.

My first two relationships were sides by accident. This was 30 years ago, and the word didn't exist. They were amazing and we are still friends. My third relationship was the turn for me. My partner at the time only wanted to top for the first two years. I was miserable every second and hated penetrative sex. After two years, he switched to bottom. I also hated topping and could barely perform. I tried it with others through the years, and never found an experience that I enjoyed.

Fast forward, I have been with my husband for 20 years now. We are both sides. I'm the happiest sexually I've ever been. It takes communication and understanding after being together so long, but it works. I would like to break the stigma that something bad must've happened to me. It didn't. I had wonderful partners and I hated penetrative sex. It's just that easy. Being a side has allowed me to truly open to exploring self-pleasure, learning, and understanding my body, and how to live a sexually fulfilled life.

**- Ted**

## The Long Road to 'Side'

I decided to come out fully when I moved to the Midwest for grad school, promising myself that I wouldn't lie if someone asked. I was in a town where no one knew me, and I had a clean slate.

I knew before this that anal sex wasn't for me. I just couldn't get over the grossness factor; that was where poop came out. How is that even sexy? Along with that, I had with a less-than-average-size penis, so I was convinced I was not an effective top. If I had to, then being a bottom seemed it would be the best option, so I tried the exercises to get used to the sensations and finding the prostate. Every time I tried, using either my hand or a dildo, the grossness factor and pain compelled me to abandon the exercise. Nonetheless, I always felt that I had to learn to either tolerate it or fake it if I was going to be part of this new life.

With dating, I always thought I would be following the traditional rituals of our straight counterparts, but I learned quickly that the gay version was hardly the romcom storyline with "Boy-Gets-Girl" being replaced with "Boy-Gets-Boy." My shyness, and being that it was the mid '90s, dictated that my only resource to meeting men was through the AOL M4M chatrooms. I quickly learned, 1) "Age, Sex, Location" was a perfectly acceptable opening line and based on those answers you were either granted a conversation or dismissed; 2) once you sent your picture or your dick size you could either continue the plans to meet or you were dismissed (the latter was usual for me if I got this far), and 3) being dismissed was "soul-sucking." I tried to move these conversations away from sex and directed them towards the "getting to know you" topics, but I eventually succumbed to the vortex of the chatroom hookup culture. Most of the time, it was a dead end, but I did manage to meet a few, usually married, men on the DL who were perfectly happy with a blow job, so any possibility of anal sex had been side stepped.

As time (and hookups) progressed, I did eventually meet other men to date (or hook up with) and I tried to be versatile, even though I believed I wasn't a top. Bottoming for the first time took a bit of trying but we were successful. Lucky for me, he knew how to be gentle enough that it was enjoyable. It was hardly "life changing" and I could tell it was not something I was going to enjoy long-term. Any other time bottoming, it was a massive (and painful) fail—I was too worked up to be able to allow entry and we usually gave up. When I took the role of a top, it was also rarely successful. I was usually more concerned of my inadequate size and that usually led to performance anxiety: I started having ED issues.

I did eventually have a 3½-year relationship with someone who called himself a "girth girl," meaning he was a bottom and he preferred girth over length. Being that I had neither, it put me at a severe disadvantage, and I obsessed with not being able to deliver on either front. He countered with he didn't have to have anal sex, he just liked being with me. Over the course of our relationship, we had successful intercourse just twice—not a great average but it was not for lack of trying. Even with the absence of anal sex, I still tried to keep things interesting with surprise midnight blow jobs or jerk-off sessions, but eventually, it became one-sided; I would give him a blow job and then I finished by jerking myself off. He rarely initiated anything, and it wasn't long before he wasn't coming to bed anymore and finding reasons to be up late. It eventually came out that we had an "open relationship" that he had neglected to inform me about. That one hurt.

Needless to say, I became single again and I went back to the hook-up culture. With the dismal failure of my last LTR, I made it clear that I was "oral only" as that was the best description to convey that the butt was off limits. I just didn't want it.

This weeded out a lot of prospects. Hook ups were hard to get and getting them was a lot more time-consuming. Eventually I was just getting whatever I could out of whomever I could get it from. If anal came into the picture (I was still trying to be versatile), I would try but fail, and then we would just get off with mutual JO … if he even wanted to stay at all. Usually, they were never to be seen or heard from again. This became my norm and for some reason I continued. I figured beggars can't be choosers.

Through all of this, I was able to figure out the things that I really enjoyed: kissing, touching, and oral. I often found myself trying to kiss and touch more than going for the crotch. There were a few who were happy to oblige but eventually they fell by the wayside as well. With that in mind, I was convinced there was something wrong with me. Being gay already made me a misfit, and now I don't fit in with the community that I thought I belonged in. So, I no longer believed I was a viable partner for anyone because of my lack of interest in anal sex.

Discovering the term "sides" was like a beam of light coming down from the sky. It defined everything I had been feeling and it has been helpful to know I'm not alone. I still have a lot of issues but at least I know I don't have to do anal … and that's ok!

- **Daryl**

## See My Side

"You should've told me sooner."

Those were the words my (now ex) boyfriend of more than a year said while he was breaking up with me over the phone. I felt like I was taking a bullet.

It struck me as a cheap shot because I'd mentioned (very nervously) my preferences to him early on when we had begun dating, and he told me he was fine with that. In fact, he never complained or even mentioned anything about our sex life up until he decided he was over us. Although I was always the one that was initiating things or looking to try new stuff in the bedroom, I was left with the guilt and the impossible burden that I couldn't satisfy my partner's needs.

He made me feel like I was broken, that something was wrong with me. That hurt and sank roots in me that I've fought hard to leave behind.

Sadly, that's a situation and a feeling that a lot of sides like me have had to deal with and will likely continue to do so. It's that fear of rejection when we meet someone new, and the time comes to tell him what we like to do under the sheets (or in a lot of other places).

Coming to terms with being a side came slowly for me. I came out in my mid-20s (I'm 33 now), and when I first started to hook up with guys I thought I would *love* to be penetrated (being a top made me too anxious to even try it and, honestly, I had zero intentions of doing it). Turned out it didn't happen. I blamed it on lack of experience and kept trying, but I was just feeling pain ... or, when I was lucky, nothing at all.

But I kept hooking up with guys and having non-penetrative sex with them without any problems. If they wanted to put it in, I usually would say that I wasn't in the mood, or rarely agree to it (sometimes hoping that this time I'd like it and other times out of guilt, I guess), then make them take it out a few minutes after because I was in pain or really uncomfortable.

The rare times I mentioned to my closest gay friends that I didn't enjoy anal sex, I was met with shock and was even shamed for it. "You have to do *something*" I was once told ... and then I proceeded to lie, saying that I was a bottom, not wanting to appear like the odd man out. It felt like coming out of the closet again, but this time people were being way less supportive.

The funny thing is, *I was having great sex*. I really enjoyed being with men and everything we were doing, and a lot of guys kept coming back so, clearly, I wasn't the only one having fun. Because I was usually just casually dating, I never felt I needed to discuss my preferences with anyone and thought that a ton of guys liked having sex in the same way I did.

It was only when one guy I was dating for a few months confronted me that I actually realized that not being into anal sex would be a real issue when trying to pursue a romantic relationship. He was the first guy that had asked me to be a top and I told him it wasn't for me. Then he asked to top me instead and I said I didn't want to do that either. We had an open conversation for the very first time in my life about my sexual preferences and I felt really heard and valued … until one day he got drunk and told me, "You didn't have real sex." We ended things a couple of days later. Since then, he apologized and he's now a big side supporter. We've hooked up multiple times since then and we remain close friends, but thinking about that night I remembered how much that judgment hurt.

The next morning, I searched online for "gay men that don't like to have anal sex," honestly just to see if there was anything wrong with me. That was when I discovered the term "side." I devoured that information, reading all the articles I could find on the matter and watching every video made about it. It was such a relief for me to come to terms with the fact the I was "normal," that there was nothing wrong with me and there were so many guys with the same preferences. I even sent the links to a few of my close friends.

Cue to the ex-boyfriend. When we started dating everything was amazing and we became boyfriends (the first real relationship for both of us) but the sex conversation didn't come up right away. I even assumed that he also was a side. But eventually, I began having this recurring fear that he would one day ask me to be a top and I would lose him for not doing it. I decided, about two months into the relationship, to talk about sex.

I asked him if he was enjoying everything we were doing, told him that I wasn't into anal and that I wanted to know if that was going to be a problem for him. He's shy and not really into having deep conversations, but he reassured me that everything was great. We were together for over a year until he, out of the blue, told me he wanted to end the relationship, mentioning only sex as the reason. I don't know if that was the real issue or just the easiest excuse. Regardless it hurt like a motherfucker.

After that day, I decided that I would never feel ashamed about the fact that I was a side and would be honest and upfront on the topic with the next guy I dated, to avoid the pain and heartbreak of being dismissed later. It can be too much to take.

Upon reflection, I've come to realize that the two main things that we as sides must deal with are compatibility issues and acceptance by our partners and peers. We already have a limited pool to choose from and our preferences make it smaller. On the one hand you will find very supportive and understanding people who will think of it as something natural, but you'll also come across those that will say that you haven't have "good sex" yet or are just confused. One guy once even suggested I go to a doctor.

I believe that, universally, dating is brutal, and sometimes I think that in the gay community it is even worse. One would imagine that after all that we have endured, we would have more kindness and acceptance towards each other. Sadly, that's not always the case.

So, to any side reading this I will offer the same advice that I'm giving myself. First and foremost, know that there's absolutely nothing wrong with you. Know who the fuck you are and all you have to offer. Never ever second-guess it or feel embarrassed about it. When you think about sex and your preferences, don't focus on the stuff that you don't do but on what you like and the pleasure that you can give to yourself and your partner. Remember there are so many ways to have sex, you just must find someone that's into the same stuff as you. Acknowledge that it's impossible to be compatible with everyone. I mean even tops and bottoms have the same issue, right? Just accept that and don't take it personally.

Don't settle until you find a supportive and understanding partner. No one is doing you a "favor" by having sex with you. You get a say in what, when, and how you have sex. And last, and maybe the most important thing: don't listen to people's negative opinions because they don't add any value to your life. People will always have something to say about any topic and you don't need anyone's acceptance but your own.

Today is a good time to be a side since the term is being included in dating apps and spreading more. I mean, you're reading a book about it! Remember to be kind to yourself, patient and to enjoy the ride.

- **Alvaro**

### Finding My Place

In his book, *Love Without Scandal. What It Means to be Lesbian and Gay,* Paolo Rigliano asks, "Is the—who does what? Or—who do you fall in love with? more important?" The question has been with me for some time in my path as a gay person, and has been a source of inspiration, provocation, and continuous reflection.

When I admitted to myself that I was gay I was already 25 years old—yes, it took me a while to admit it and even after I did, I struggled a bit to feel part of the diversified gay community. I've always had the feeling of being a "minority within a minority" even if it wasn't clear to me why. At first, I thought it was because, although I consider myself a nice guy, I don't have a very handsome body (I'm rather thin, 55 kg.). Then, I began to realize that it could all depend on my sexual preferences. I've never had full intercourse, so how could I define myself? Virgin? Or at most qualify under the convenient label of "versatile?"

When I opened up about this to a few friends, they looked at me with amazement, and some with disappointment and pity. But, when one of my friends directed me to your "Sides" article on Grindr, I swear it was liberating for me. Discovering that so many of us think the same way was really a great relief. It was like suddenly opening my eyes and making a second coming out: I'm gay and I'm side!

I love sex like crazy, but for me it's also romanticism, intimacy, tenderness, complicity, being able to cultivate a relationship with my partner that goes beyond sex, including respect, equality, sharing, attention and caring for each other.

When I joined your Side Guys Facebook group, for the first time I felt like I was in the right place—fully welcomed, supported, and understood. And beyond the group, I think there are really a lot of us out there! I think the side phenomenon is really underrated and much more widespread than we might imagine. You can love, be loved, and feel complete in a thousand ways, beyond prejudices and stereotypes. I am very happy we now have greater visibility.

Perhaps it won't always be easy to be welcomed for who we are and who we love, even, paradoxically, in the gay world. But this isn't a reason to feel incomplete, undone, inadequate, or defective ... far from it! Within our gay communities we can provide an example of how to reflect on the quality and value we really want to give to our romantic relationships.

Finally, I'll borrow the words attributed to a Saint Augustine of Hippo, which seem very apt to me: "Love, and do what you want!" ...well actually they remind me of Lady Gaga too!

I thank you again for everything you are doing to make us sides more visible and understood.

A big hug, have a nice day!

- **Matteo**

# Being a Side in Rural India

It was 2017, the year before homosexuality was legalized in India. I was a 19-year-old college student on a residential college campus and began dating my then boyfriend. I had told a few close friends I was gay, but he was closeted.

Importantly, we had no access to sexual healthcare. Hell, we weren't even able to access condoms in the remote area where our campus was located.

After the first night out with my boyfriend, I immediately texted one of my close girlfriends living in another city. I told her that we had gotten intimate, and how excited I was. "Was the sex good?" she asked.

"We were just intimate," I replied, "We didn't do that part (anal sex)."

"Why not? I'm sure you both aren't infected given that this is the first time for both of you. So, what's the problem?"

"We weren't just very confident about doing that. You know, why take the unnecessary risk?"

"I get it," she said. "Those tissues (meaning the ones in the rectal lining) are delicate and could pass on infections easily. Well, glad that you guys had a great first time. I'm so happy for you!)"

We were together for more than a year. I often wonder how we pulled it off for that long in rural India, one of the most unsafe settings for two gay guys. Living through those intense situations made me appreciate the different layers of getting intimate with somebody. I didn't date much for the next four years after that relationship, but I realized that I was fine without anyone penetrating me. Our sexual health could've directly impacted both of our future lives. Choosing to have an unorthodox sexual life without penetration was our best bet, and the most beautiful thing was that we were never dissatisfied with that experience. I know that I have and will always enjoy a sex life that doesn't involve penetration!

Health is wealth and an invaluable asset for all communities, not just the gay community. And sex is an activity that involves not just two souls, but two bodies with complex biological designs. We tend to forget our vulnerability, as our bodies are beautifully sensitive and imperfect. Not all bodies are okay with all kinds of physical touch and realizing that made me feel comfortable with the word and the concept of "side."

The beauty of the queer community is redefining standards. We've set so many noteworthy milestones, including same-sex marriage and gender-diverse recognition. Why, then, don't we also try and contribute to redefining sex and intimacy, and dismantle various inequalities on an interpersonal and intrapersonal level in our societies?

Exposing the concept of "side," not just to the gay community but even to the public, is a steppingstone towards immense social progress. I strongly believe in that!

**- Sander**

## Who Am I Becoming?

As long as I can remember, I have felt different.

I have had profound hearing loss and visual impairment since childhood, and it limited my ability to be with people. Birds, plants, spiritual research, and reading kept me busy. I could spend time with animals without fear and experience emotions and life with them, and this became a form of rehabilitation. Thanks to them I eventually reached people.

When I was 9 or 10 years old, I discovered the company of some adult and well-balanced men, and I began to get an inkling of what it felt like to be normal. During my adolescence, my parents, who didn't talk to me about sex, secretly put sexual education books on the family bookshelf. The title of one of them stuck in my mind: *What Every Boy Should Know*. Even then I was deeply aware of sexual taboos, so I always tried to put the book back exactly in the same place it was so no one would notice I'd looked at it.

My sexual initiation happened with a friend. I was about 12 years old. The boy lay down on me and we rubbed stomachs and genitals against each other. I experienced an explosion of emotions and orgasm and panic, overwhelmed by my sexual feelings. I pushed him off and jumped out of bed. Later, I couldn't repeat the experience of that pleasure.

Sometime later when I was in high school, a friend showed me a local sports center where men looked for sex with other guys. I was terribly embarrassed. Then I met an older sunbathing gentleman and silently sat down next to him to masturbate with him. However, he wanted to have anal sex with me. It was painful and overwhelming, and I asked him to stop "attacking" my integrity. Ever since, I have felt a deep aversion to such sex. Later, I heard about gentlemen meeting in the city toilets, but for a long time I wasn't brave enough to visit them. Eventually though I got hooked on clandestine gay meetings in toilets and city parks, finding forbidden love and friendships at the beginning of the '70s in socialist Poland.

There was no gay literature or organizations in that country, so I learned on my own how to function in a parallel reality. It was a relief to sometimes meet nice and helpful guys among this crowd of sexual predators. But virtually everyone wanted anal sex with me. I was lonely so I allowed it, always clenching my teeth in pain. I felt like a tool in the hands of lovers, but I justified my partners' actions, believing their ignorance and sexual imprinting was different than mine. After all, most of us were/are deeply wounded by the social conventions and the toxic patterns in the gay environment! I thought that type of sex was necessary, that guys couldn't live without it.

My relationships with partners faded away, due to "unacceptable" sexual behavior and emotional domination, among other reasons. At times I allowed myself to be top but didn't feel the big satisfaction I felt during my young sexual initiation. I don't know how much time and energy, at the cost of my studies and later scientific work, went into the search for friendship and love in the gay world and in myself.

Searching for partners often resulted in unpleasant situations. I was blackmailed and beaten by hooligans. Once a policeman stopped me and threatened that if he would find me again at one of the gay meeting places, he would notify my employer. A large part of the gay community did not accept me due to my impairments, my persistent lack of consent to anal sex, and my refusal to use various stimulants. I tried to adapt to the expectations of both heterosexual and gay societies. Was seeking others' acceptance my main need? Did it result in a partially unconscious break in my own integrity? Unexpectedly, heterosexuals helped me achieve self-acceptance. I learned that hearing loss, vision problems, etc., are just dysfunctions and nothing else. My strong interests in biology, scientific work, and the search for the nature of human beings helped me to be on the surface of life, not in its dark depths.

Life is a kind of experiment, just like research, and brings so many unexpected questions and answers which probably will continue to modify my functioning. One such discovery was finding a description of myself when I found the Side Guys group on Facebook!

I've often wondered about the role of birds in my life. I guess it's about inner freedom. Birds represent it by moving through the air even over the longest distances. My experiences of discrimination and indirect awareness has shown that protecting my inner freedom is the essence of life and power. I now am almost 66 years old, and I have a partner with whom I've now been together for three decades. A few years ago, he moved to another part of the country, but we are still together.

What have I learned in all of this? That it is crucial to hurt others as little as possible. Even now I still see a lot of social shortcomings in myself, but I feel so grateful to the Universe for these experiences and wouldn't change anything.

**- Nick**

## A Reason for Hope

As I approach my 50th birthday, I've recently been thinking back about major developmental turning points that have ultimately defined much of who I feel I am and how I see myself. I've learned that the source material for who I am has always been there as long as I can remember, it just had to be uncovered or experienced in order to shape me.

While most of it has been positive growth, a few things have left lifelong scars I'm not confident will ever go away. Three of these turning points come to mind: The first was discovering the gay person I think I knew was always there, lurking under the surface, but didn't reveal itself until I was nineteen. I had sex with a few girls in high school, but I felt like an imposter. I had always liked and fantasized about seeing adult naked men. I played around sexually at age 6 with an older male babysitter and liked it. I had a few crushes on older men, usually mentors. In hindsight, enough signs of being gay were there.

I didn't experience any self-loathing during my realization and transition period. Growing up in a small town of a few thousand was the hard part. I felt an overwhelming sense of being entirely alone for more than a year, seemingly an eternity at that age. Pre-internet, it wasn't clear how to meet other gay men. During that period, I never did much to hide it from my family and they have always been supportive ever since finding out when I was in my early twenties. I eventually met other gay people, but that soon became a second defining trauma for how I learned to hate myself and how I felt others related to me. The first sexual interaction with another man left me feeling comparatively undeveloped sexually. I had hoped it was a fluke but guy after guy was largely (literally) the same experience. Worse, a few men expressed disinterest upon us both disrobing, or they would urge me to service them and then they'd excuse themselves.

My partial solution was adopting an "I don't hook up" mentality, and I mostly held to that. However, even non-sexual gay social situations—every drag show, gay party, or gay bar experience—were not exempt from repeated messaging that bigger was better, so it was hard to find much of a community…or alternately, laughing-stocks with "not-worth-it" equipment. Even an LGBTQ hiking club, which seemed like a safe haven, had an organizer lamenting to me that the "the kid with the huge dick isn't here today."

Overall, I have been particularly struck how being gay has historically put us at odds with the rest of the world, and yet here the local highly visible/vocal gay men had implemented a caste system to further marginalize a subset of us. So much for inclusivity.

The final "aha" moment happened just a few months ago (June 2022) when I was describing my sexual interests after someone was confused about what I liked sexually. It seemed they thought I wasn't interested in anything at all since I didn't list any of the conventional things he thought constituted sex. But at least they gave me a word for it when they said, "Oh, you're just a side. Yeah, we won't have anything in common." I hadn't done any research into exactly what a "side" was, but it instantly clicked in my mind.

After some reading, I may have a bit of a "beef" with the term "side" though, even if I think I generally get it and am functionally not alien to the concept of being something other than a top or bottom. If it isn't presented carefully—and I don't feel that it always is—it's easy for it to come across as still being a list of activities that may feel exclusionary to people who are only interested in the minority of activities listed. Or at least, that is my fresh impression of some of the things I've read. The descriptions that I feel work best describe it as what a side isn't—we aren't tops or bottoms and we don't have penetrative anal sex.

So, I don't know yet where my "side" journey will take me. I'm still somewhat hopeful that awareness about sides at least makes it easier for me and others to engage in a discussion up front about what sexual practices we may or may not be comfortable with. And particularly to have any requirements or preferences not be treated as defective. I'm hopeful that I can finally feel like I belong somewhere and can be appreciated and accepted for who I am.

On the other hand, I had already felt that being gay has severely restricted me to a minority of the population for potential partners. On top of that, being perceived as sexually inadequate further restricts my pool of potential partners. So far, I'm undecided as to whether the discovery of being a side is the coup-de-grace (death knell) for me having any chance at all for future sexual activity, or whether it opens up the ability to find "like-minded" men where I find some sexually comfortable space to thrive in.

I'm truly hopeful that it's the latter.

- Jeff

## Stalemate

We were four years into our relationship when my partner told me—awkwardly, embarrassedly—that he no longer enjoyed our sex life. Sometimes, he continued, he'd thought about breaking up with me because the sex was so bad.

It was especially painful to hear this because I loved the sex we had. In fact, it was the best sex of my life. After years of living alone and hooking up with strangers, I was constantly amazed by our lovemaking, how it could be both familiar and exploratory, tender and aggressive, gentle and passionate. I'd never had anything like it before, and it seemed to be getting better as each year passed.

I'd been assuming that Michael felt the same way. It shocked me to realise that he didn't, that he felt bored and unfulfilled. It was humiliating. I felt totally stupid.

But then, if I was honest with myself, I had sometimes— over the preceding months—wondered whether Michael was loving it all as much as I was. He had sometimes seemed rather absent emotionally as we lay next to each other, and sometimes appeared just to be going through the motions. But I'd brushed all that aside, thinking that he was probably tired after work, or that maybe (hopefully!) I was just imagining it. Now I was confronted with the reality of our situation.

Michael didn't need to spell out what the problem was. It was obvious. For me, sex was about kissing, hugging, closeness, and lots of other things but not (or rarely) penetration. For me, penetration spoiled sex: it added complication, it created anxiety, it was a task to perform rather than an expression of love or desire. I didn't want any of that. But I'd always known deep down that, basically, Michael was a top. He'd been happy up to a point to go along with what I wanted, but it didn't fully satisfy him. I guess, to him, it was as though we did the foreplay but stopped before the real thing. It was as though we were two college roommates jerking off together. It was a bit of fun, but it wasn't real sex, not what real gay men did.

I also knew that sometimes—very rarely—I did feel in the mood for penetration, and I agreed to bottom. And then Michael came alive: his eyes lit up, his body tensed, he became hyper-alert and focused, like a predator fixated on its prey. Suddenly he was fiery, exuberant, energized. Then when it was over, he would smile from ear to ear and kiss me with deep gratitude.

And of course, it thrilled me to see him like this. I always, after the event, vowed silently to myself to do more of this for him because it made him so happy and, in turn. it brought out a side of him that made me happy. I would become a better bottom for him, I decided. I would try harder, get over myself. So, I searched online for articles and books about bottoming, I bought butt plugs and dildos so I could get used to the feeling of being penetrated, I tried different types of lube hoping that one of them would ease the awkwardness.

Then after a few days I'd settle back down again: I'd return to normal and so would our sex life. Michael allowed that to happen. He was too nice a person to press the issue, to insist on what he really wanted. He knew that anal wasn't really for me, and he accepted that, obviously hoping that, if he waited, just occasionally I would relent and let him go the whole way. So, we would carry on as before, and once again—after a while—I would begin to feel his emotional absence, his boredom.

Our awkward conversation was a year ago. Michael and I are still together, and we're still at a stalemate during sex: he wants to fuck me, I want to do everything else. Sometimes we can meet in the middle, mostly we can't. Sometimes we try to communicate about it, mostly we don't. I don't know whether we'll stay together or not. I hope we can find a way to work this out, because he's the love of my life and my best friend.

I feel that I'm letting him down, not being able to offer him what he needs, but then I've spent most of my adult life feeling that kind of thing about the people I sleep with. Until my mid-twenties I never did penetration, and people generally thought that was weird. Eventually I decided to go for it and become a top, which resulted for the most part in lots of awkwardness, lots of losing my erection, lots of apologies and lots of concerned and confused looks from my dates, who then never contacted me again.

Eventually I decided that it wasn't going to work, and I reverted to not having anal sex. Again, it provoked negative responses. I remember (a typical scenario) one young man who, early in our date, asked whether I was top or bottom. When I replied that I didn't do either, he looked annoyed and frustrated and asked me snappily: "What's the point of all this then?!" He felt I'd been wasting his time, and we abruptly parted ways.

I started bottoming when I started dating Michael because I knew it was important to him. I remember, early in our relationship, he showed me with glee the roll of about 100 condoms he'd just bought. He was thrilled... I was horrified! It turned out that, for me, bottoming was at least more pleasurable than topping, but ultimately it just didn't feel right, it wasn't what I wanted.

I used to think that I wasn't masculine enough to be a top, but actually I think I'm quite masculine in my own way. If anything, I think that, for me, sex is the place where I can briefly relinquish my masculinity and settle into a more archetypally feminine state of emotional openness and connectivity. So yes, if the mood strikes me, I can somewhat enjoy bottoming if I think of it in terms of receptivity.

But more generally this means that I don't want any penetration of either kind. I don't want to *fuck*. I want instead to explore my partner's body, and for him to explore mine; I want to become sensitive to touch, I want to hug, kiss, play, fool around, have fun; I want to feel closely connected and held. Some people could achieve all this through anal sex but, for me, anal sex gets in the way. Penetration for me isn't play, it's work.

I've spent a decade thinking that there's something wrong with me and trying to improve my sexual performance. Now I'm trying to accept myself more. Regardless of what happens with my relationship, I'm a "side," and that's OK.

- **Tom**

## Not Really Gay?

I was 11 when I first realized I was gay. I'd been aware of being interested in guys before then but after seeing two men living together in a TV soap and having a "normal" relationship it suddenly clicked that the feelings I was having were more than just an urge to see and touch another guy's dick.

At that age most people have had some sex education and are aware of the basic mechanics of sex between and man and a woman but, of course, sex between men wasn't something that was discussed in schools. It was illegal here in the UK under section 28, which "prohibited the promotion of homosexuality by local authorities" and was only repealed in 2003, when I was 17.

So how two men had sex was something of a mystery, and my naïve brain certainly didn't consider anal a possibility.

Once again it was left to television to inform, the UK series of *Queer as Folk* aired for the first time when I was 13 and introduced the idea of penetrative sex between men to me, and I remember at the time thinking that it held no appeal for me.

Eighteen months later, in high school, I'd become friends with a guy named Peter who had come out as gay the previous year, which led to questions being asked about my own sexuality. I'd told my best friend back when I was 11 and, to his credit, he was cool about it and never told anyone else. But now I was having to deny it every day which was becoming exhausting, so I took the plunge, told my closest friend first then started to answer truthfully when I was being asked "Are you gay?"

When I told Peter I said that although I was sure I was gay I didn't think I wanted anal sex, his response was "Oh, so you're not a real gay, just a tourist." I didn't know it at the time, but I'd just been treated to my first bit of side bashing.

Not long after this another guy, a friend of a friend named

Chris, and I became close, and one thing led to another one afternoon in my bedroom. It would prove to a bit of a false start. I got nervous and stopped it after he pulled his dick out and ordered me to suck it.

A couple of months later my parents suggested I could invite someone on holiday with us. I asked Chris and he eagerly agreed. Since our false start we hadn't mentioned what happened but the night before we left whilst he was staying over, he suddenly gets on top of me and lays out his plans.

"Tonight, I want us to get naked and lay pressed together under the sheets, nothing else just feeling our bodies together. Then over the next two weeks I want us to try everything."

That's how things played out, the first couple of days it was just hand jobs before moving onto blow jobs, all of which was very hot and good fun. On day four the topic of anal came up. He was very keen to try it and despite my reluctance I agreed to give it a go.

Topping, it would turn out, was a no-go for me. I just couldn't maintain my boner so we decided I would have to be the bottom. I should add that we were both naïve and unprepared—no condoms, no lube no preparation.

We went at it for some time and whilst it wasn't horrible, it was underwhelming. There was the excitement of "I'm losing my virginity," but the act itself was kind of nothingness. Neither one of us came and afterwards we decided to stick with the other stuff, much to my relief.

Once the holiday was over, we continued in a "friends with benefits" arrangement until the end of the year. Despite being happy with this I couldn't help but develop feelings for him. When he started to date a girl with whom we were mutual friends I put a stop to it.

The following year I entered a relationship with another guy, things were fine for a while with just hand and mouth play, but the pressure to go further was increasing. Eventually I relented and gave it another go. This time we were better prepared, and I thought it might make a difference. I'd convinced myself that it felt good, and I'd start to desire it. But it wasn't to be, despite several attempts each time was as underwhelming and unappealing as the first time I'd tried. I reached a point where I didn't want to do it again.

It became obvious he was unsatisfied with this, and he began to resent me. Towards the end we had a conversation where he told me I would have to get over it if I ever wanted a real relationship and he was bitter that he'd be going to university still a virgin because I wouldn't top him. Our relationship soon ended.

Another guy came along. It was an odd relationship that built up slowly, and there was no sex for a long time. He'd text me, telling me he had so many fantasies and desires but never went into detail partly because I didn't push it, fearing those fantasies would all be anal-related. He was deeply closeted and or meetings were mainly outside, he wouldn't come to my house in case we were seen together, and word (somehow) got back to his family. Eventually we had one experience together—a hand job—after which I let him know that anal wasn't something I wanted. He didn't have much of a reaction at the time, but he stopped taking my calls and replying to my texts from that day.

I had been with one guy or another from the day I came out, but then I had a couple of years of being single, occasionally meeting random hook ups who didn't mind just having hand or blow jobs. During this time, several people told me that I wasn't really gay. I was accused of being a time waster and asked if there was something wrong with me. It was a brief period in my life where I wondered that myself, my ex's words about never being in a real relationship without anal haunted me.

One day I started Googling "gay men who don't do anal" and I came across the term "frottage" and a site dedicated to those who practiced it. It sounded interesting but the key was many of these men didn't do anal and I felt a sudden relief not to be alone. I began to search for guys who mentioned it in their profiles, finding a few but often on the other side of the country.

Then, a woman I worked with kept trying to set me up with a guy she knew. After initially resisting I agreed to let him have my number. Shortly into our first face-to-face meeting he announced he wasn't into anal. "Oh, thank God!" I cried. "Me neither."

We are still together 16 years later. It was sheer luck or coincidence, or maybe even fate. I consider myself very fortunate.

**- Alfred**

## Too Long in the Making

I am a 66-year-old gay white male, a psychiatrist, single, and have never been interested in anal sex.

I came out just after finishing college, and just before the HIV crisis began. Fortunately, I had a support group at the University Gay Center which was based far more on friendship and biweekly dances and parties than on sex. Nobody there ever pushed me into unwanted sexual behaviors. When I began medical school, we learned early on about the sensitive anatomy of the rectal areas, tissues very close to blood vessels and easily perforated. That information alone convinced me I was not very interested in anal sex, especially not when HIV began.

After finishing my training, I lived in San Diego and attended a progressive church that attracted the LGBT community and, sadly, where we witnessed illness and death of many gay male members — presumed "bottom" partners. I also lost a good friend of mine to HIV who was a "bottom" and who traveled for work all over the country meeting men for sex.

Later I experienced confusing encounters with other men.

I recall one where I'd been at a gathering, met a guy, and went with him to the apartment of a friend. We became intimate but soon he became rageful that I didn't submit to anal sex. I didn't know how to explain this to him and just left. There was another incident in Rehoboth Beach, Delaware, where I went with on a night walk on the beach with about five guys and became attracted to one of them. We did cuddle but then he explained to me that if a guy did not begin trying to initiate sex with him, he assumed they were bottoms and would "start looking for their butt hole." He said he understood that I was not into that type of sex, but I never heard from him again.

Over the years I began making excuses for avoiding anal sex such as, "I never do this the first time," or just ignored the whole idea and proceeding with other behaviors. Most of the guys thought this was foreplay and enjoyed it. I also compensated by becoming involved in non-invasive mild kink, which turned on some guys, but again they usually expected it to lead to anal sex. I did meet some guys on social apps devoted to kink that didn't expect sex, and recall reading a book in a gay bookstore in San Francisco that said for some men, the kink play was "the full meal." At least I felt a bit validated in my behaviors.

Later, while living in Honolulu, I met a guy at the gay running club. He said he was conservative sexually (essentially a "side") and that worked well for both of us. We were together for about a year, and he even followed me back to San Diego. However, he was clearly homophobic and always hiding. Despite my appeals to go to a community coming out-group, he was not interested in getting out of the closet and went back to Hawaii.

I recall speaking to a gay psychologist about the challenges of being a side, and he suggested reaching out to younger guys and guys that weren't out long and who may be receptive to non-invasive sex. This began a series of my meeting gay men who were open to side intimacy but were not secure about their sexual orientation. This led only to short-term encounters as my partners' fear of intimacy precluded meaningful relationship. Until Craigslist stopped posting personal ads, it was a good place to specify exactly what I wanted, and I met some men for side activities.

While in therapy, the idea of joining Facebook groups came up, and I encountered the Side Guys group and Gay Men's Brotherhood. Then Grinder and Scruff started a side option. Now, I am very open about being a side, but am frequently asked if I am a "top or bottom." Most guys still think everything else is foreplay. When I make it very clear what "side" is, most are not interested. However, occasionally a guy will say that he's also a side. I met one guy like this while on vacation, which was a good experience. It does seem like the gay male community is becoming more aware of personal choices, and more open to side guys.

I wish this change had come sooner for me. I harbor no fantasy of ever being in a long-term relationship.

- Marty

### The Five Ps

I thought being gay was the hurdle.

That perhaps, once I'd had those often-fraught conversations with family and friends, once I was out and proud, I wouldn't need to keep any secrets or have anything about me that was different or taboo. But once I cleared that hurdle and found myself in the bedroom, I realized something was still off. Put plainly, intercourse didn't top my list, and I had to get to the bottom of it.

Just like being gay, I understood I was a "side" before I'd ever heard the term for it. It was indisputable, this preference for non-penetrative sex. It wasn't a fear of intercourse, or even a strong aversion. So, I thought it was my issue, and gamely topped and bottomed with a few guys before admitting to myself and my partners that the experience did absolutely nothing for me. I think I can explain what I mean by using five Ps: **Prowess, Pleasure, Pain, Porn,** and **Power**.

The first, **Prowess**, guided so many of my hookups from a nervous teenager to now. Regardless of my sexual ability, I was anxious to show off what I could do! I'm good with my hands, with my mouth, with my speech, with my touch. I can go fast or slow, gentle or demanding, long and lazy, short and sweet. But to me, intercourse is rote. Rhythmic, but unchanging. A means to an end. You don't have to be good, just a pole or a hole. Boring, who needs it?

The same is true for **Pleasure**. I noticed when hooking up that partners were the most responsive, the most vocal, the most "eyes rolling back in your head," when one or both of us was actively doing something. Jerking, sucking, grasping, pinching, licking, stroking, etc. It's as if intercourse put us on parallel but separate tracks. "I'll keep doing this until I finish, you just keep laying there." Or "Don't mind me, just pound away." Where's the fun in that? What is participatory? I know some guys derive incredible pleasure from these experiences, but not me.

**Pain** is the difficult part to address here. I'd never want to be the recipient or provider of pain to anyone in my bed, but for many intercourse encounters, that element was undeniably there. The first time I had intercourse, I topped (at the request of my partner at the time). We'd been having a heretofore incredible time together. Our hands and mouths and bodies together felt incredible. Then the copious lube was applied, and I saw him tense before anything touched anything. It wasn't sexy, it was upsetting. I asked him what was wrong, and he assured me nothing was. He just wanted to be "ready" for me. We went slowly, him urging me on, and I saw genuine pain cross his face. I won't forget it. He continued to guide me and began responding appreciatively, but any pleasure he may have experienced was eclipsed for me in those moments of what I could tell was genuine pain. Likewise, when I would bottom for a partner, the initial discomfort was always greater for me than any stimulation of my prostate. Even when the supposed "spot" was hit, it was that Peggy Lee song, *Is That All There Is?*

A quick detour to **Porn**. Are you like me, reader? Do you fast-forward through the fucking? That should have told me right away that intercourse wasn't for me. I don't even enjoy it in fantasy. Hot guys getting naked, kissing, touching each other, having oral sex, that can be really hot to watch. But what do I care if they start humping like rabbits? To me, a fantastic porn star dick disappearing into a fantastic porn star ass is right when I lose interest. Just me?

Finally, being a side really is about **Power**. I don't mean dominance or submission in the bedroom (though that's fun too). I mean it's about agency. About saying to your partners what you want and what you can provide. No apologies, no equivocations. Taking a man in my mouth feels incredibly powerful. Bringing him to the edge and taking him over. Giving of myself and feeling that intimacy in return. I don't think that's about topping or bottoming or anything else. That's about trust, connection, strength, and vulnerability. We all deserve that, for ourselves and our partners. Any journey towards that is worth it, hurdles be damned.

- **Joe**

## Wandering in the Dark

Like many young boys growing up gay, I initially had a narrow view of sexuality, it was an ordeal as I had always struggle with the sensation that I had been forced into the role of bottom and being submissive. My friends would define me by how I acted, how I behaved. It was a role imposed on me at a very young age.

Before I even found about the term "side," I had already

suspected my sexuality revolved around something like that. As a kid and a young adult I struggled a lot trying to connect with other gay peers. Deep down I never actually resonated with their experiences (I still believe some are still trapped in that dynamic and haven't found the courage to accept that penetrative sex can be too traumatic for some). But like many other human things we do, they've normalized their trauma. This isn't a judgement, though, just something I wonder if it's happening in their minds.

I remember the first time I told my friends that I did not like being penetrated and that I believed I was a romantic person who liked everything else but penetration. I remember the constant stress whenever I wanted to have sexual intercourse with someone I'd met but was already concerned about getting to the actual part. I tried topping several times only to find out that seeing the pain reflected in the other person's face would only make me feel bad and instantly lose any sexual desire.

This was a constant issue with me for several years. It even drove me to believe I might not have been gay, that maybe discomfort during penetrative sex was a clear indicator that I was confused.

I started trying to find ways to provide pleasure for my sexual partners that could work as a loophole so that I didn't have to resort to engaging in anal sex. I would try to satisfy them in many other ways so they could climax before they suggested penetrative sex. That way I would feel okay since we would finish before getting to that part. But all this only made it worse for me. I started to see sex as something that I had to do rather something I enjoyed. I ended up thinking I might have been some sort of asexual person.

The truth is, not having a clear way to identify my preference had me constantly tumbling from label to label in hopes that I would find one to shield my practices and not feel so judged.

This lack of clear definition of who I was even led me to

lose friendships and drift away from places I enjoyed. At the time the friends I had were heavily involved in several activities that gay guys usually end up doing due to a lack of restraint and usually due also to our overall marginalized status—but that's a topic for another time. I would visit often and even end up working in dark rooms, clubs and using illicit drugs to "enjoy" the many pleasures LGBT nights can offer (in some places). I thought that by me (and my friends at the time) being involved in this scene, I would eventually come through. However, for a young person who didn't fall in either role as top, bottom—or vers for that matter—these scenarios only made it worse.

One of my lowest points was when I started using illicit drugs to numb myself, and let men do to me things I didn't enjoy. Looking back, I can't believe the extent to which I went just to try and have a "normal" gay experience, but at that time I had no idea that "side" was a choice.

My breakthrough, however, came from the very dark place in which I had buried myself. In between the confusion, I found someone like me, someone lost to the lust that dark rooms and heavy drugs parties attract. At the time I worked these parties as a barman to earn extra money. This allowed me to have access to the areas where men would fuck in little cabins. I saw this guy wondering aimlessly, I guess in hopes to find someone or for someone to find him. I liked him and followed him into one of the cabins. We shared glances and started kissing. He undressed and hugged me. I thought that was weird at first—such a gentle approach, no immediate lust, no forced interactions. We were both on something— "candies" and "pills" that get passed around to feel "the love" in the air—but we hadn't decided to act on lust, so we did the most anticlimactic thing you could imagine: we fell asleep kissing and embracing. In hindsight I think we might have been overwhelmed by the drugs we had pumped into our bodies to "enjoy the party," but this interaction felt correct, like what I wanted from every interaction.

Every performance anxiety was gone. We just felt comfortable enough to not do anything we didn't feel like doing, and when we did a series of maneuvers to climax, I felt it was the most satisfactory experience I'd ever had. When we both came, he suggested we cuddle for a little longer before leaving (I was working at the time and thought that probably people had started to wonder where I was. However, one of the benefits of working in these environments was that you're cloaked by the chaos).

He left the cabin, and once again I followed. I never saw him again in that way, but a few weeks later I found him on social media, and today we still are friends from afar. Soon after I had to move countries, and I think for him it might not have been such a special, liberating experience as it was for me.

It made me understand that not all men are looking for the same experiences, and that maybe this was a form of sexual contact some people crave— a valid sexual encounter with just the male touch and love without the penetration.

Some might see sex as something that if certain parameters aren't met, then it's not valid. This was what my former friends used to think. They would tell me I wasn't getting proper sexual experiences because I got too much into my head. But the truth was, I had never liked being penetrated by casual strangers.

A few years later I came across the term "side" and it reassured of what I had already defined for myself. It felt wonderful as it finally had a name. But more than that, it was a keyword to identify a bigger community. I found new connections, men who related to my experience, men who were also into the things I was. I must say I come from a small country in Central America, and thus finding like-minded people has been hard, but not impossible.

I'm currently traveling to various destinations, meeting people, and enjoying life, no longer pressured to participate in sexual activities I don't enjoy for the sake of getting some half-pleasure out of it. It took some time to arrive to this version of myself, but it has definitely given me hope for the future.

- **Gregory**

## What a Pain in the Ass ... Am I Right?

I am a 44-year-old, white, cisgender, gay man. I also identify as mostly a versatile side. That means sometimes I engage in anal sex, but eighty percent of the time I enjoy "outercourse" rather than "intercourse." I am also someone who has experienced *anodyspareunia*. What is that you ask? It is a pain in the ass, literally. Anodyspareunia is the clinical definition of severe and persistent pain during receptive anal intercourse. For more information on that, I highly recommend looking up Dr. Simon Rosser's research on the topic.

I grew up in a Catholic household with a Catholic school education and no discussion of sexuality. The only messages I got about sexuality were a short puberty video in the 8th grade, my pediatrician told me I shouldn't "play with myself," and a half-year-long health class taught by the football coach, who did not want to be there! I didn't think I was supposed to talk about sex, so I didn't. It wasn't until I went away to college that I started asking questions. Thank goodness I did. I didn't have my first orgasm from masturbation until I was 18 years old because I thought "the clear stuff" was the end. Imagine my shock and embarrassment when guys in college told me that was "pre-cum" and to "keep going." Most of my information about sex came from my peers.

When I came out of the closet in 1998 as a gay man, I had minimal information on gay sexuality. I only knew I was attracted to men. Again, I relied on my peers to help me during this time. I learned that above all, anal intercourse was a big deal in gay sexuality. Many people asked me if I was a *top*, *bottom*, or *vers*. I had no idea. What confused me was that people told me that anal intercourse hurts as a bottom, but that didn't match up with what I saw in porn videos. The bottoms always seemed to enjoy themselves. And if it hurt, why did so many people do it? I was confused.

In my mind, I saw bottoming as "losing your virginity," so being a good Catholic boy, I wanted to wait for the right person before I bottomed for the first time. Until then, I explored and enjoyed other sexual activities such as kissing, body contact, mutual masturbation, oral sex, and external anal stimulation. My peers gave me the impression that I was missing something by not having anal intercourse. It was important to me to do that with someone special and I was willing to wait.

When I was 20 years old, this handsome man asked me out on a date and asked if I was a *top, bottom,* or *vers.* I told him I hadn't ever bottomed or topped and was waiting for the "right person." Later, he asked if *he* could be the "right person." He said he could see us having a wonderful future together. He took me back to his place and we engaged in all the sexual activities I enjoyed thus far. Then he asked me if I wanted to bottom and I said yes. He was patient and kind as he explained what he was doing. I could tell I was nervous. The pain started immediately when he entered me. He was kind at first, but then when I said we should stop, he didn't. He told me to give it a minute and kept fucking me and I didn't say anything because I remembered that other people told me anal intercourse hurts. Maybe this was normal? Eventually, I couldn't stand it any longer and I pushed him away and said I had to go to the bathroom. He said, "I wish you didn't stop. I was so close to finishing." I was embarrassed thinking I did something wrong. He said it was fine and we would try again another time. I helped him orgasm and then he told me, "It's late. You should leave." I saw him one more time at a social event and he barely acknowledged me. That hurt even more.

Since then, I have rarely enjoyed being a bottom. My pain level has usually been too uncomfortable to finish. Because of this, I decided to switch positions to a top. While this was less painful for me, I found myself preoccupied with what the other person was experiencing and nervous that they were in pain and not telling me. My erection usually would catch on to this, realize the focus was not on him and exit stage right. Now it was hard for me to desire and find pleasure while bottoming *and* topping. Whenever someone would ask me: *top, bottom,* or *vers*? I would say I was a top but avoided telling people I didn't desire anal intercourse or found it pleasurable, because sometimes when the mood was right, and Aquarius was in the seventh house, anal intercourse *was* pleasurable for me. Unfortunately, this strategy yielded awkward and unfortunate sexual situations. I wished that *neither* was a viable option. I thought there was something wrong with me.

When I started grad school for sex therapy, two important things happened: I learned about anodyspareunia and I learned there was more to anal intercourse than *top, bottom,* or *vers*. There was also *side*. My professor assigned an article to read where I learned about painful anal receptive intercourse. Wait! I wasn't alone and other gay men also experience the pain I was feeling? I also learned that anal intercourse isn't necessarily *supposed* to be painful. This was very affirming to me and helpful. Around the same time, I heard someone call themselves a *side*, or someone who doesn't desire or find pleasure during anal sex. I was flabbergasted! For the first time, I had a seat at the table and had a choice when it came to anal intercourse.

This information has been a game changer for me in how I see myself and how I negotiate sexual situations. As I said before, I call myself a *versatile side*. Using the concept of a restaurant as a metaphor, I communicate what *is* on the menu, rather than what is *not* on the menu. Kissing, body contact, mutual masturbation, oral sex, and external anal play are very popular menu items. Rave reviews! If they ask for anal intercourse, I let them know that it isn't guaranteed on the menu and if that is what they are truly hungry for, this might not be the restaurant for them. This has empowered me to communicate the sexual acts I am excited about offering, while also managing expectations about my sexual boundaries and recognizing that other people have different appetites … and that is okay! In doing so, I find myself more comfortable to offer anal intercourse in the middle of a meal when it is available as an option.

As I look toward my sexual future as a versatile side with anodyspareunia, I am *grateful* that I have language to use as a map to guide me. I have the *wisdom* that I am not alone in my journey. And I have the *courage* to walk the path towards my sexual pleasure.

- **Ivan**

## Living Sideways

Growing up in the mid-'70s as a teen in a borough of NYC and having a gay brother made me no stranger to the idea of man-to-man sex. Aside from what I'd call the kid stuff — "I'll show you mine if you show me yours," I hadn't experienced anything truly interactive until I was thirteen and a half. Very young. I was within walking distance to the large commercial area with department stores and the like. Oddly instinctively, I lingered in a store bathroom and received my first blowjob from a man. It felt great! I was freaked out and guilt-ridden, but it became the start of my sex life. I explored other "tea rooms" by day and at night would sneak out and walk to this big cruisy municipal parking lot. I was out there at fifteen! As a cute chicken I could just lay back and enjoy oral sex. I didn't have much interest in anything else. My secret world gave me a rush which became part of the sexual experience for me.

In my later teens and early twenties, I got more into reciprocal oral, both in cruising places and dating. I considered myself a "practicing homosexual" — not a boring partnered gay like my brother. In college this bottom wanted me to top him. The idea turned me off. I had been with some women in high school and said that was the real thing. He disagreed but couldn't convince me.

(A quick footnote here: It would literally be decades before I understood the power of the prostate and would occasionally allow play there.)

I liked kissing, frottage and body contact a lot but no ass play, except maybe for getting rimmed sometimes, but I was always hesitant for any kind of penetration. I thought it would hurt and felt literally dirty to me. But I thought if I found a man I really loved, I would let him fuck me. My first true love, Carlos, was a little older though we never had anal sex consensually. I was in my early twenties and new to the NYC drug and party scene. We took something one night and went out with his roommate. I was in and out of consciousness, but I believe overnight my boyfriend penetrated me with a roommate egging him on. The next day I was very sore. He denied it. I've always had vague flashbacks of that night, and really, that's the one and only time I've had anal sex.

By this period, we were well into the eighties and the AIDS crisis in NYC. Like many, I was skeptical, confused, and then worried. Carlos and I had broken up and then he got sick. I managed to get a T-cell count test from a doctor doing a study I was volunteering for and was assured I was okay. I told myself that the cruisy sex I was still having that didn't involve any anal, was sort of a saving grace for me. I felt like "Safe Sex" was already my playbook! I continued to cruise rest areas, tea rooms and parks for sex.

As for the "what was I," early on I had to identify as a top because I certainly wasn't a bottom or versatile. Giving oral sometimes provided me the element of submission. That could be hot.

As the internet entered our lives and cruisy AOL chat rooms, I often described myself as "not a bottom but I suck cock like one." To me this meant I would be into pleasing a top, just not by bending over for him. Most guys found this confusing. I'd often be told in chat and sometimes in person, "We're both tops and two tops don't go together so…" and that would be that.

I can't recall the first time I fucked a guy but, in my twenties and thirties I sometimes would. I usually found the bottom to be either boring or having more fun and me doing most of the work! I didn't like condoms which made it easier to avoid topping. Casual dating and cruising allowed me to continue to stick with oral, hand jobs, kissing, body contact. I was fine with this. Over time I added adult video arcades, the occasional bathhouse, and cruisy YMCAs. I was able to get my sexual needs through cruising, although I later realized I was a sexually compulsive.

In my late thirties I found a man I am still with after twenty-five years. I fucked him a couple of times but otherwise it was oral, touch, mutual. We went through a brief phase of "experimenting" with couples and three-ways, but it never included anything off my list. I did discover the joy of nipple play at that time and that was a nice addition.

After a second move to a major city, I decided to start doing male massage, having often been told of my great touch. I started on Craigslist and eventually a male massage site. I offered a "sensual massage with erotic elements." Many of my regular clients were straight and married. These sessions were sometimes sexual. Most wanted a release at the end which could be by hand or orally if I chose to.

I would usually allow oral on me. Some would want anal sex. As I was getting older, I became fearful of maintaining an erection for anal. I avoided it and would often "mount them" and simulate penetration with my finger in motion. Some never knew!

Topping me was not an option. I'd allow some to simulate it lying on top of me. I will say it's a turn on to have man's body on top of me; being kissed on the neck: a feeling of giving up control. Like many clients, I grew up believing the man was in charge. There is something to surrendering — even in a vanilla fashion. Letting go. I believe that there are few instances in life when we allow ourselves to be so physically vulnerable as lying prone on a bed naked. As a side, I've had to explore activities other than fucking to experience this.

Through my fifties and now early sixties, I still have no desire for anal sex. Nipple play has become more central to my sexual enjoyment and as an "older" man, much of my connection is via video chat and the occasional visit to a cruisy spa or bookstore when traveling. Online I will sometimes roleplay as a top or bottom if someone asks; and that can often be fun. Younger men I am not invisible to generally want that dominant daddy-top thing which can be hot. It supports the idea that much of the turn on of sex is in our heads anyway.

I have often felt like an outsider not identifying as top/bottom, especially since gay porn presents archetypes that carry over into the community. But I accepted being different years ago.

"I am what I am and what I am needs no excuses."

In a culture of invisibility for gay men as we age, of new labels and acceptance, discovering the term "Side" has made me feel finally at home in a way. It's been validating and good to see and read about other men who identify similarly. It's a movement. Let's go!

- **Terry**

### A Fellatio Fanatic

It was the late '60s. His name was Bruce. I was nine, he was nine and little did I know he was about to "facilitate my very first sexual experience" (as opposed to the heteronormative term of "taking my virginity!")

My father was in the military stationed at Scott AFB in Illinois and he and his family were visiting from Philadelphia as our fathers had been college roommates. While our parents laughed, drank, listened to James Brown and Aretha Franklin, and played pinochle in the living room, and our sisters played with Barbies in my sister's adjacent bedroom, we retreated to my parent's bedroom to watch TV. I still have no recollection whatsoever of how it all started but the next thing I remember, he opened my pants and started to play with my penis. My father had a tie rack on the back of the bedroom door and the next thing I knew my back was up against the door with neckties falling over my head and around my shoulders, and Bruce was on his knees sucking my dick. I don't remember how long it lasted (and surely at that age, I didn't ejaculate) but I do remember that warm sensation, the likes of which I had never before felt. I reciprocated and recall liking the feeling of his dick in my mouth. But from that moment on it is fair to say I was obsessed with oral play and had officially begun my journey to becoming the fellatio fanatic I am today!

Fast forward to sixth grade. I had a classmate named Courtney whose father also was stationed at the same base. We became the best of friends and he would come over to play after school. On base we lived in a four-apartment building that had a shared laundry room. I remember one time when he came over, I told him "I want to make you feel good." He said "how?" I told him to pull down his pants and sit on top of the washing machine. He complied so I gave him his first blow job and after swearing to secrecy, he said he looked forward to the next time. So was I.

My next experiences came during the formative Boy Scout years and let's just say I was a very popular tent mate! I remember blowing a fellow scout named George who was the son of the scoutmaster, using part of the oath to swear our secrecy. It was at tent episode the following year that I was about to have my first confrontation about my experiences with boys. A couple of neighborhood kids and I were sleeping out in the backyard one night and I asked one of them if I could play with his dick. I was twelve, he was ten, and at first he said no, but then changed his mind. Little did I know that he went back and told his mother that "I had put my mouth on him." His mother told my mother and the next thing I know I'm sitting in some counselor's office with my mother basically embarrassed and denying out of sheer fear that the episode ever took place.

In the high school years, I used to play around with another kid in my neighborhood (the "all-American Catholic altar boy") who was the same age but we went to different schools. We were messing around one afternoon in my basement and he asked me to fuck him. The concept was very foreign to me but I said I'd try it. Without any sort of lubrication other than the proverbial 'spit,' I got a little way in before he started to put up some resistance. Maybe it was the lack of a real lubricant but I distinctly remembered that I did not enjoy it at all, but he didn't want to stop. I'm sure we probably tried again on another occasion. Ironically, he ended up joining the police force after college … probably on the vice squad no less!

College was a major turning point as I was fully coming into my sexuality. I had zero interest in women other than as friends or confidants. All of my sexual experiences were with men, especially after discovering the bookstores, bathhouses, and glory holes which were oral sex heaven – so many tokens, so many dicks, so little time! DC's notorious Glorious Health and Amusement Club was almost my second home for many years. My closest gay friends and I pretty much had an underground secret gay society. It was the mid to late '70s and none of us were "out." That was back in the day when you'd test the waters by saying you were bisexual and, dependent upon the response, only then would you declare your real orientation. The talk was always centered around feminine things like "getting my pussy pounded," and "I need some Vitamin D (dick)." There was excessive use of female pronouns to address each other ("girl," "Miss Thang," "Queen," and she/her) but I was never accepting of that terminology to refer to males and I definitely was not getting fucked. There seemed to be this unspoken competition with women for the acquisition of men or "trade" as we called it.

But I was not a "girl" and men didn't have pussies; I was a man who was sexually into men and therefore everything masculine. I pledged a nationally renowned black fraternity as a test of my manhood because there were no masculine gay role models for me to emulate as I came into my sexuality. On one occasion, I decided to see what all the hype was about, I got drunk and let a fellow band member try to fuck me. He was the drum major in the band and let's just say he had a pretty big "baton!" It lasted all of about 15 to 20 seconds and I knew it was not for me. Sadly, all of those who chastised me for not being into anal sex, about not being "authentically gay" back in the '70s and '80s, are no longer with us as it was the heyday of the AIDS crisis. I lost so many friends. In some strange cosmic way, I owe my life to oral sex.

I came out in 1986 at the age of 30 and the reaction of my family was very loving and supportive. This gave me the foundation for being an advocate in the gay community back when we were only two letters: G and L! I worked at the G/L Hotline at Whitman Walker Clinic here in Washington, D.C., was a volunteer when the AIDS Quilt was laid out on the National Mall in the '90s and have marched in my share of equality parades. However, with the onset and recognition of this wonderful side community after 37 years, I have found my true identity. This second coming out is about validation and having a place at the proverbial table. Formally changing my "category" on most apps has been an empowering experience, confirming that our community is not monolithic and that our preference of sexual activities does not define us. But for me, it finally provides relief from the historically stereotypical expectations normally imposed on me not just as a gay man in general but a black gay man specifically. With a newly enhanced identity, I am optimistic about my future!

- Warren

**The Courage to Tell My 'Side'**

"I feel closer to my side self than my gay self sometimes. As we all know it takes a huge courage to come out as side in front of other gay men because it invites multiple judgments, trauma, and it results in isolation. But is it all about being depressed? I don't think so. I really had a wonderful sexual compatibility with one of ex partners. He often says that it has always been exciting and thrilling to engage in "side-sex" with me. Often, I heard people cribbing about how romantic and sensuous it is to be touched and felt with erotic tenderness and even if they don't engage in penetrative sex, they'd call themselves anything except "side." I stay in India where many gay men would shame sides as being sexually inactive or unattractive. I have broken friendship with few of them as they have suggested me to be a "top" just to increase my body count.

There have been extreme breakdowns I had when I have been just reduced to a disabled body for not participating in the penetrative gymnastics. Moreover, there are people who don't even know the meaning of "side." Some would just throw out your opinion based on their normative thinking.

I have seen there is already insecurity and frustration amongst gay men. Being a side has doubled it for me. After the break ups I have never found someone suitable for me. When I clearly state my preference, people will never date me. Some will just be friends but never consider me as a lover.

Now, I have also met people who aren't into penetrative gymnastics, but they won't call themselves "sides." I find it weird but that has been an open reality in gay spaces of India."

**- Raj**

### An Unwritten Rule?

As a gay man, growing up in the late '80s wasn't easy. Gay liberation still had quite a way to go. The AIDS epidemic was raging, and amongst all that, finding an identity had its challenges. Being "out" in the workplace was certainly ill-advised for many, and even amongst family and friends one just couldn't be sure. On top of that, identifying as a "side," a term not coined until decades later, presented what seemed like a frustrating and insurmountable obstacle. Yet, in hindsight, it was probably a good way to be, considering what we now know about HIV.

I'm not entirely sure where my aversion to anal sex originated. Or did it have an origin at all? Just like being gay, it may simply be the way I am. It just never interested me. Even during my initial ventures into porn, some years before my first experience, I found it annoying. Is that what it's going to be like? Kind of straight sex with a twist?

Being on the cuddly and affectionate spectrum, it seemed redundant to me. My dislike was confirmed when my first boyfriend attempted it. He was quite the top and believed I was a seasoned bottom. That painful experience imprinted on my mind much like a newly hatched duck follows whatever object it sees first. I was young and eager to please, so we stayed together for two years. However, the aversion and discomfort never subsided.

When I started insisting on anal-free activities, seeing other guys was hit and miss. Some just left, others went along … begrudgingly, mind you … but by far the most common response was something along the lines of: "So, what do we do then?" I could think of plenty of very enjoyable things to do. Gay culture, however, even to this day, seems to be fixated on penetration. An unwritten rule I somehow missed? By then I had many doubts about who I really was. Was I genuinely gay or just a straight man who doesn't like sleeping with women? My attraction to men, though, was never in dispute. That newly hatched "duck" my mother gave birth to obviously had a male midwife!

One day I met a very handsome man in one of the underground nightclubs. On the way home, I pondered how to break the news to him. He was such a good catch that I even considered letting him do it. The flood of testosterone took precedence over rational thinking. But I needn't have worried. About an hour later, as we lay next to each other, somewhat exhausted, I casually mentioned the absence of anal sex. His reply surprised me: "No, I hate anal anyway. Glad you didn't insist." That was a kind of a hallelujah moment for me. I wasn't alone or weird after all. I kissed him gently on the forehead and said thank you. "What for?" he asked. "You have no idea," I whispered in his ear. We saw each other many times in the months following until he had to return to his home overseas.

Sometime after that I met my second partner. We were introduced by a friend we had in common. Although there was a sexual attraction from the start, we just stayed friends for about six months. Neither of us wanted to make the first move. When we finally slept with each other, we discovered our side preference was mutual. That may have been part of the reason we eventually fell in love, but I don't think love is that easily defined. Our relationship lasted more than ten years, and we never ventured into that territory, nor did we miss it. Some guys may say we never had sex in those ten years, something I fiercely dispute.

As life would have it, another man came into my life and we separated amicably—not one of my proudest moments, but love is a beast that's impossible to tame. We met at a dance party, and it was one of those love-at-first-sight stories. As we grew older and got to know each other, the love grew exponentially. He came from a relationship where he was expected to be the bottom. We tried a lot of new things sexually, as you would expect when you feel very comfortable with someone. To my surprise, I discovered, for example, that I quite enjoyed being dominated. We had so much fun experimenting that we forgot about the anal stuff. I wasn't the one to bring it up, but it eventually reared its ugly head. Well, ugly is a bit unkind; dreaded is perhaps more appropriate. Awkwardly fumbling with condoms, a requirement in those days, we did it. Given his role in his previous relationship, I was the top this time. I think it was the second or third time when I gazed into his eyes and saw a sort of distant or vacant look.

"You're not enjoying this?" I asked.

"Not really," he replied.

"So why are we doing it?" I asked.

"I thought you wanted to," he said.

Whatever I said was just an echo. We then decided to go back to the fun stuff we did before. We never looked back. That was 22 years ago. Our sex life has been as fulfilling as anyone could wish for, even to this day.

Close friends often want to know who is the top and bottom in our relationship. When the inevitable answer is "Neither," there usually is a long pause. You can almost see their brains processing that information: Are they joking? Once they realize we're not, someone always predictably asks: "So, what do you do then?"

Human sexuality is such a vast and diverse field. We often don't realize it until we let go of the many stereotypes that somehow have manifested in our culture. Anal sex is but a small part of it, yet it can easily overshadow the many other possibilities if we believe it to be obligatory.

- **Charles**

### Coming Out All Over again

For me the process of defining myself as a side has spanned two centuries and has evolved. I began exploring my sexuality during the AIDS epidemic and I adopted a practice of having primarily oral and non-penetrative sex partly for my own protection but also because anal sex is so intimate for me, and I preferred to do it with a committed partner.

I was married and in a monogamous relationship beginning in the year 2000 and I would occasionally top my husband because he enjoyed it and I wanted to please him.

He passed away a year and a half ago and now I feel like I am coming out all over again as I look for new partners. In the past I had met guys at bars, and we had gone home together and figured out mutually enjoyable things to do and it seemed fine. Now, however, this is primarily done on apps where there seems to be an assumption that someone is going to penetrate someone else, and a person better know which box to put themselves in and be quick about it. It's been disheartening.

I go with "side" now that there is a box for that. It helps with hookups and I'm so grateful there is a term and an option for that in the checkbox world. If I were to find myself in a relationship again and it pleased my partner for me to top him I probably would, but the world of oral and tactile sensuality is much more satisfying for me and is my preference.

**- Paul**

# Conclusion

As you can see from these stories of men who have finally discovered an identity as "sides," they have often felt lonely, marginalized, or ostracized by other gay men. Some still do. You may even see yourself in some of these stories.

My sense is—and I've said this many times in my books and seminars—this is because too often gay men haven't done their personal work to mature themselves, to evolve. Maybe during their formative years, they absorbed certain attitudes and ideas. Maybe they have taken on an identity that conforms with their particular clique and are afraid that if they step outside of it they risk becoming "othered." Unfortunately, they've insulated themselves from new ideas or thoughts. Let's face it, we all have a deep-seated need to "belong," and if someone falls outside of this "group think" phenomenon, it is easy for others to point a finger at them for feeling or thinking differently.

In my decades as a therapist, and even over the years I've been writing this book, I've seen a disturbing movement in the gay community toward replicating heterosexual norms. In other words, we've become more and more top/bottom-heavy, recognizing fewer nuances between that supposed "gold standard." I attribute much of this to the rise of social media, more dating apps, and more porn. When the public discussion increasingly is framed around just two choices—or at least fewer choices—it becomes more difficult to think outside this box.

I was fortunate. Even in my 20s I didn't feel the kind of loneliness many of these "side guys" have talked about. Rather, I was always on a mission of sorts to find someone who wasn't into penetration and who had the same desires I had for a different kind of intimacy, who valued relationship more than penetrative sex. If someone I met insisted on penetrative sex, even if I imagined that they would otherwise make great partners, I just pushed them aside when they rejected me. Eventually I found Mike, my partner for three decades now. Perseverance pays off.

The gay community may have something to learn from those in the kink community. They make their preferences clear up front, whether it is BDSM, fetishes, or whatever. Very often they are not into penetrative sex, and don't value orgasm. These are *not* an expectation in that community. They say what they want without being impacted by the values of vanilla culture. That seems emotionally healthier to me.

Can we sides be this confident to claim our identity? I'll say it again: Sex doesn't have to look a certain way. *We can decide.* Gay men in general need to be more open to the idea of outercourse instead of intercourse.

I've found that even within the sides community there are those who insist on terms like "orthodox side," meaning that someone doesn't fit into the category if they may get off on using toys or fingers or rimming, but not penetration with a partner.

Can we all just stop with the judgments? The expressions of sexual pleasure are *infinite*!

My idea in writing this book was to let readers know that there is nothing to be ashamed of. If you're not into something, you're *just not into it*. Same goes if you're into something that someone else isn't. Let's just grow up and accept people as they are.

You are not damaged goods because you like something that others don't, or don't like something that others do. As the many guys who've discovered the Side Guys Facebook page, *there is no normal*. You want what you want. If someone else doesn't want it, move on. Don't feel ashamed, just keep looking. You are not alone, Mr. Side Guy.

Stand up for who you are. To put it another way (pun intended), keep your chin up and your ass down.

# Citations

Angelini-Cooke, E. (2022). The effect of gender role conflict on help-seeking attitudes for men who have sex with men (MSM) and men who have sex with men and women (MSM) with painful receptive anal intercourse (Order No. 29163451). Available from ProQuest Dissertations & Theses A&I. (2659210502). Retrieved from https://www.proquest.com/dissertations-theses/effect-gender-role-conflict-on-help-seeking/docview/2659210502/se-2?accountid=29103

Bollas, A. (2021) Masculinities on the Side: An Exploration of the Function of Homosexism in Maintaining Hegemonic Masculinities and Sexualities', Sexuality & Culture. https://doi.org/10.1007/s12119-021-09848-3

Bollas, A. (2023) Men, Sides, and Homosexism: A Small-Scale Empirical Study of the Lived Experiences of Men who Identify as Sides, Journal of Homosexuality. https://doi.org/10.1080/00918369.2023.2208250

Farber, J (2022) Rise of the sides: how Grindr finally recognized gay men who aren't tops or bottoms. The Guardian, June 20. https://www.theguardian.com/technology/2022/jun/20/rise-of-the-sides-how-grindr-finally-recognized-gay-men-who-arent-tops-or-bottoms. Retrieved March 19, 2024

Hellman, R.E. (2019) The way of the world: How heterosexism shapes and distorts male same-sexuality, a thesis, Journal of Gay & Lesbian Mental Health, 23:3, 349-359, DOI: 10.1080/19359705.2019.1620066

Hellman, R. E. (2021) Male homosexism: A concept in search of acceptance. Sexuality & Culture, 25, pp. 337–346. https://doi.org/10.1007/s12119-020-09744-2.

Kort, J (2013) Guys on the 'Side': Looking Beyond Gay Tops and Bottoms. https://www.huffpost.com/entry/guys-on-the-side-looking-beyond-gay-tops-and-bottoms_b_3082484, Apr 16. Retrieved March 19, 2024

Pearson. K 2021 Sex Myths That Experts Wish Would Go Away. https://www.nytimes.com/2023/10/15/well/family/sex-myths.html

Printed in Great Britain
by Amazon

52761823R00046